FOREVER BEGINS WITH A KISS

WARDHAM BOOK 9

ZOE YORK

ZOYO PRESS

FOREWORD

This book is a departure in writing style for me—for the first time ever, I'm including "point of view" scenes from characters who are not the hero and heroine of the story. As anyone who has been caught up in the swirl of excitement that is a big family wedding knows, there are often other stories going on around the happy couple's nuptials —and for *this* wedding, two of those other stories are the start of a new adventure. So there are snippets in between Chase and Mari's story from their siblings, Audrey and Sam.

This story, *Forever Begins With a Kiss*, is the second last book in my Wardham series. Wrapping up this series is bittersweet, but it's time. The next novel, *All That They Desire*, will conclude the story lines introduced in my very first novel, *What Once Was Perfect*. But it won't be the end of romance in this small town, not by a long shot. If you want to read more about Audrey and Heath and Sam and Gillian, as well as their friends and a whole new generation of people falling in love, look for my next series set on the shores of Lake Erie: **Whisper Beach**, coming soon.

For now, enjoy the little side dramas that happen when two people throw a massive party to celebrate their love—and how none of it matters nearly as much as how they maintain their special connection when everyone else is occupied. Chase and Mari are two of my favourite characters, and revisiting them was a lot of fun.

As always, you can keep up with my books by joining my newsletter, or Facebook reader group!

All the best,

Zoe

DEDICATION

the whole is greater than the sum of its parts

For the InkHeart Authors, a wonderful collective I was proud to be a part of

WELCOME TO WARDHAM

A sleepy village on the shores of Lake Erie, ready to explode with passion...

Between Then and Now - Carrie & Ian Nixon (#1)

Their story didn't start with a fairytale romance. Their marriage wasn't chosen for love. But they still chose each other...time and again. *a novella*

What Once Was Perfect - Laney Calhoun & Kyle Nixon (#2)

He was her first love, and she's always owned a piece of his heart. *a novel*

Where Their Hearts Collide - Karen Miller & Paul Reynolds (#3)

When the girl next door meets the man of her dreams...at exactly the wrong time. *a novel*

When They Weren't Looking - Evie Calhoun & Liam McIntyre (#4)

She's not looking for love, he's not thinking about forever. It's not what they expected. But it might turn out to be just what they need. *a novel*

Beyond Love and Hate - Beth Stewart & Finn Howard (#5) *

First comes love, then comes marriage... Or maybe just a single night of passion, no strings attached. (Yeah, right!) *a novella*

No Time Like Forever - Chase Miller & Mari Beadie (#6)

It started with a kiss... *a novel*

Perfect No Matter What - Laney & Kyle Do Vegas (#7)

A business trip for Kyle and a last-minute rearranging of

Laney's schedule provides the perfect fantasy escape to re-focus on what really matters. *a short story*

Beneath These Bright Stars - Evie & Liam's Wedding (#8)

It's time for Evie & Liam to say "I do". *a novella*

Forever Begins With a Kiss - Chase & Mari Get Hitched (#9)

Chase and Mari tie the knot in the middle of Mari's first big tour. *a novella*

All That They Desire - Evan West + Jessica Dornan + Brent Dornan (#10, coming soon)

Nothing about love is easy. *a novel*

———

* Finn Howard's brother, Ryan, lives in a town a few hours north of Wardham. If you like this series, you'll probably love Pine Harbour as well: small town military romance with heroes you'll fall in love with.

Pine Harbour

Love in a Small Town
Love in a Snow Storm
Love on a Spring Morning
Love on a Summer Night

READ LOVE IN A SMALL TOWN FOR FREE!

ABOUT THIS BOOK

Before they can say I do, they need to say enough...
Mari Beadie's singing career is on the rise, and too often, she's flying in the wrong direction from her ex-NHL hockey star fiancé, Chase Miller.
Chase prefers to stay at home in Wardham, where he's gingerly getting involved with local politics.
Neither of them is happy, and the ridiculous wedding being planned by the entire town isn't helping matters. It's time to reconnect—with the door locked and their clothes off.

WARNING: This book overflows with sexy hockey players, frothy wedding details, and frivolous sex scenes. And it's not just the bride and groom who are getting lucky!

1

____

The lights in Ak-Chin Pavilion dimmed, and the Phoenix, Arizona crowd roared.

Chase Miller knew that sound in his bones. It had been two years since he'd heard it, and it hadn't been here, in this outdoor concert venue, but close enough to make his gut tighten with anticipation.

Now he was just one of easily twenty-thousand people cheering for the next act. He grinned. He was pretty proud of the songwriter about to take the stage, so it was a good thing everyone sounded excited. Otherwise he'd have to knock some heads together.

The sun had just finished setting to the west, and the heat of the day was fading into a comfortable late summer warm night. Perfect for an epic concert, and the crowd was buzzing with excitement. The opening group had been a local band with a sizeable following, so even though most people were there to see Alaskan Nights, the headlining act, they were in a good mood and happy to be entertained by the Canadian riding the middle of the playbill.

Her first chord happened in the dark. Then a spotlight lit up centre stage, where she was perched all by herself on a stool. Long, dark waves spilling over her shoulders. Giant smile. A girl and her guitar.

"Hey y'all!" she called out. "I'm Mari Beadie. You havin' a good night?"

Chase surged to his feet, hooting and hollering before settling back in his seat. Even though she was a hundred feet away, this was the closest he'd been to his fiancée in three weeks, and that was reason enough to make a ruckus—even if it wasn't usually his style. That she was about to play her biggest concert ever? That called for a wolf whistle and him pulling out his phone to take a video. Maybe five.

"My guy lived here in Phoenix for almost a decade, and every time I visit, I'm stunned at how beautiful it is here. Makes me a little...jealous, especially in the winter." She flashed a quick smile then dipped her head as she strummed the familiar opening strains to a top forty country song about envy and desire that she brought her own edgy, angsty vibe to—Chase was biased, but he thought her version was perfect.

It needed to be. She only had five original songs, about to release on her first EP, and her set as the middle act called for nine songs. So she was kicking off with two covers, before sliding in to her own stuff.

He could still hear the warble in her voice from four months earlier, when she'd curled up in his arms and talked out which songs she wanted—and which songs the label had approved.

They weren't always the same.

As an ex-professional athlete, Chase got the circus element of the entertainment industry better than most people Mari trusted. He tried to use that knowledge for good and not evil—it would be too easy to snuff out the bright spark of excitement at her first record deal, her first tour, with his well-earned cynicism about celebrity and performance and business.

"Wow," she breathed into the mic, lifting her head for the first time since she'd started singing. "You guys are fun to play for, I'm telling you. Okay, so that was good to get the first song out of the way. Because…I need to tell you a secret. Are you ready?" Another grin, and Chase was pretty sure his heart was going to explode. Cynicism be damned. "This is the biggest crowd I've ever performed in front of."

A huge cheer went up at her admission, but Chase only cared about the tiny frown between her brows. He wanted to smooth it out.

He should have called her when he landed. He didn't because she'd turned into a superstitious performer, with a rigid pre-show routine, and he didn't want to knock her off her game.

Rookies were often like that. Hell, some league all-stars were still like that at the height of their careers. He got it.

"This next song was written by a good friend of mine, Bren Getson, who was supposed to be here tonight..."

Chase leaned back in his seat as she started to play.

Life had a funny way of working out. Here he was, back in Phoenix, where he'd played NHL hockey for nine years, and he was sitting on a hard plastic seat, watching his soon-to-be wife perform for a crowd of thousands. A lucky break she'd gotten because she shared a label and a manager with Bren, who'd needed to bow out of the tour because he was having surgery on his throat.

It meant their wedding would take place smack in the middle of the tour. She'd only be home for five days before flying out again, but when she did, he'd go with her for a few days. Honeymoon on a tour bus.

When Chase left the NHL, he thought his days of buses and planes and living out of a suitcase were done. The joke was on him.

He didn't mind that this was possibly the rest of his life. Most of their time would be at home in Wardham, in the new house they'd built on the lake—he'd even built Mari a recording studio so she didn't need to fly to Toronto or Vancouver or Nashville to lay down tracks.

But when she needed to tour, or travel for promotion or collaboration...either he'd go with her, or meet her on the road.

Sometimes as a surprise.

He grinned to himself. This had been a good idea. When Mari got home, it would be go, go, go. They wouldn't have a ton of time together, but tonight once she was done, they'd be alone. Thousands of miles from mothers or sisters or best friends. One very persistent bridesmaid who was both a sister and a best friend. And a self-appointed wedding coordinator.

Audrey wasn't going to let him have a moment alone with Mari until their wedding night. So if he had to fly to Phoenix to make some quality time happen, it was the least he could do. He'd used his contact in the Coyotes media office to get him a ticket to a sold-out show, and now Mari was one song away from being his for the night.

As she started strumming her guitar for a ballad about finding home, he quietly got out of his seat and headed for the exit. He'd have the best luck getting back stage by finding a roadie that knew him rather than trying to get past the local security guard.

At the bar, someone did a double-take and called out. "Hey!"

If it were anywhere other than Phoenix, Chase wouldn't have even slowed down. This didn't happen to him much anymore. He hadn't been a huge hockey star to begin with, but in Phoenix the odds of being recognized were better than anywhere else outside of Wardham. This had been his city for nearly a decade, and fans were the engine that made it possible for professional athletes to play the game they loved at the highest level. He nodded back. "Hey, man. Great concert, eh?"

"Yeah..." The other man searched his face, trying to remember who he was looking at. "You're....You used to play hockey here."

"Sure did. Loved being a Coyote. Always will be, man." Chase held out his hand and they shook.

"Man, this is cool. They traded you, right? To the Rangers?"

And just like that, the bro-bonding moment was over. "Sorry, bud. That was Petr Gunterson."

"Yeah. Big blond guy." The fan—Petr's fan, maybe—squinted, then turned red. "Oh. Shit. My bad."

"Hey, don't worry about it. Names don't matter as much as scores, right?"

"Sure...hey, I *am* a fan!"

Chase just smiled and nodded. He didn't mind, but now he just wanted to get backstage. "Howl on, my brother."

The fan turned away. You win some, you lose some. It didn't matter, in the end.

He pulled the VIP badge Mari's manager had mailed to him out of his pocket and slung the lanyard around his neck. A security guard stood by the crew entrance, but Chase didn't even need to explain himself before a big, tatted-up guy with an impressive beard caught sight of him.

"Well, fuck right off, if it isn't Mr. Hockey in our midst."

Beard Guy waved off the security guard and held out his hand as Chase stepped through the gate. "Steve Brand, crew manager. We met briefly in Toronto, but I recognize you from Miss Mari's bunk on the bus. We didn't know you were coming out to visit."

"It's a surprise, actually. You think you can help me get backstage?"

"Absolutely."

The other man led him through a maze of instrument cases and set boxes, up a metal staircase, and into the wings of the pavilion's bandshell. His heart thumped a little heavier as he followed Steve into the dark shadows.

With a whispered thanks and a quick handshake, he was left standing next to the roadie who would take Mari's guitar as she walked off stage—and into his arms.

On stage, she lifted her gaze to the sky and belted out the last line of her song. The lights fell as the audience exploded, and Chase had to squint to see her hop off the stool and skip toward them.

"Here you go, Mike." She blew the roadie a kiss as she handed over the acoustic guitar and did the sexiest fist pump in the air, right in front of Chase.

And then she saw him.

"Ahhhh!" She leapt into his arms, and he braced his good leg and his core, catching her with arms he worked out every day for moments like this—because there was no way he wasn't going to catch his bride when she was flying through the air at him. "Chase. Oh my God. Ohmygod."

She peppered his face with kisses and he squeezed her tight. This felt right. Worth every second of air travel and every amused glance they were surely getting right now from the crew.

"What are you doing here?" She exhaled roughly as she slid down his body, keeping her arms around his neck. "Wait, I don't care. You're *here*. I've missed you so much…"

She trailed off, just shaking her head and grinning at him.

"Hi." They both laughed at his single word answer. He pressed a quick kiss to her mouth, then glanced around. "Is there somewhere private we can go so I can do the R-rated version of this greeting?"

Her eyes flared wide and her lips parted. Oh yeah. They needed to be alone and pronto.

Mari had already been flying from the performance. The adrenaline rush was insane, and it seemed to grow in proportion to the audience size. Normally she partied a bit with the VIP guests and called Chase to give him the run-down. Sometimes they had a bit of phone sex if she had a private dressing room. Sometimes she fell asleep on the tour bus, amped up and horny, wishing her man was there to do all the filthy, celebratory things her imagination could conjure.

And once in a blue moon, when she was very, very lucky, he showed up and swept her off her feet.

"Come on," she whispered, weaving her fingers through his. God, she wanted to jump his bones right there, in the shadow of twenty-thousand people who'd just given her a standing ovation.

But public sex wouldn't fly with Chase—and when she came down from her adrenaline high, it wouldn't work for her either. Of course, right now she'd drop to her knees and rip his jeans open.

She wasn't safe out in the open.

Flagging down the stage manager, she pointed in the direction of her dressing room, then grinned broadly as she pointed at Chase.

"They know what we're going to do now, don't they?" he growled in her ear as she shoved her dressing room door open and he crowded against her back.

"Wait until our wedding, and our parents are going to know and be grinning about the fact that we're going to get it on."

"Don't be a buzzkill, baby."

"Is that possible?"

He laughed and shook his head. His hands were everywhere, stroking up her belly and cupping her breasts, and roving over her hips and across the tops of her thighs, which felt awesome, but she was coated in a totally unsexy layer of sweat.

"Shower," she gasped, twirling in his arms, trying to get past his octopus hands to lock the door.

"Second round," he mumbled as his mouth descended on the skin at her neck. "Door sex first."

Now it was her turn to laugh, albeit weakly. "I'm not crippling you just weeks before the wedding."

Chase was one of the fittest men she'd ever met—and even more so because he was training for his first triathlon. But he'd been in a career-ending car accident two years earlier, and still do physiotherapy for his left leg. He'd use a cane for a year, and when it rained, he still had a slight limp.

If she'd had a thought in her head when she first saw him backstage, she wouldn't have jumped on him.

And from the dark way he was glowering down at her, he was thinking about the same things—but coming to a very different conclusion. "I can hold you up."

Desire warred with concern, but the restless, heady thrum of hormones pulsing through her body would give in. She was weak and she'd missed him so much. Swaying against him, she let out a hungry little moan.

"Or..." He flashed her a wicked smile as he shifted his stance, sliding his bigger, broader body against hers, turning them both until her back pressed against the door —hard and unyielding steel against her back. Extra-hard and equally unyielding man flooding all her senses in front. She watched through lust-drugged eyes as his beautiful lips curved even further. "I could spin you around and fuck you from behind. Bend you over and make you scream."

Oh, yes. Hands shaking, Mari undid the button on her jeans and unzipped her zipper. Chase's hands closed over hers, his back curving tight against hers.

"I can do that." When she nodded roughly, he kissed her neck in approval. "Good girl. Hands on the door."

Ahhh. Her belly tightened in anticipation as she did as instructed. One of his palms flattened over the swell of her bare skin right above her panties, fitting into the open vee of her jeans. The other skated higher, stroking up, up, up until he found her right breast underneath her shirt. Squeezing her swollen, aching tissue through her bra, he worked her up with his fingers at the same time as his words. He whispered how much he'd missed her and how amazing she'd been on stage. She rocked back against him, helpless to give back but still wanting to work him up the way he was playing with her.

"Fingers," she gasped as he squeezed her tighter.

"Where?" He nipped at the curve of her ear and she turned her face. She meant to kiss him, but she froze when she saw the look on his face. Lust, yes, but the deepest kind. Layered with so much love it stole her breath.

"Inside me," she whispered, closing the gap between their faces. Their noses brushed as she exhaled softly against his lips. "And I think you promised me an X-rated kiss."

He grinned and tugged her hands free from the door,

turning her around again. "Kick off your boots. It was only an R-rated kiss, but I'll make an exception if you ask me nicely."

"Pretty please with a cherry—" His mouth crashed onto hers, cutting off her words. His teeth scraped against her lower lip and his tongue stroked deep, strong and hungry as he claimed her mouth. Against the small of her back, the door was cold, and that sensation spread as he tugged her shirt up, baring her bra. With only a bit of flailing, she managed to kick off her cowboy boots, sending them flying as she danced on her toes. And still he kissed her.

He devoured her whimpers as he removed her bra and palmed the weight of her breasts, teasing her nipples in hard, desperate peaks with his thumbs.

He licked away her pleas for him to go faster, instead slowing down and wedging his thigh between hers. Through two layers of jeans, she could still feel every throbbing inch of his erection, reminding her she wasn't the only one who'd been going without. Not the only one who'd missed this connection terribly and needed this rough, demanding scrabble to satisfy that itchy hunger for one's mate.

And finally, when she was halfway gone toward a panting, begging dry-hump-induced orgasm, he finally broke away from her mouth and dropped to her knees. He kissed her bare belly as he tugged her jeans and panties off, leaving them in a heap on the floor as he surged back to his feet and lifted her up in the same motion, his hands sure and steady under her bottom.

He wasn't leaving any room for argument. At some point, he'd undone his own jeans and shoved down his boxers. Between them, his cock bobbed free and eager, and Mari didn't need to be told what to do next. She reached between them and slid him into place between her slippery wet folds.

The first thrust took her breath away. It had been too long and as wet as she was, he still took some adjusting to. But the ache as he pulled out was even worse and she rocked her hips, desperate to be filled again. She wrapped her arms around his neck and lowered herself onto his length, moaning softly as he stretched her all the way that time.

"Again," she whispered, grinning against his mouth.

Up and down she rode him, slowly at first, then faster, until he pressed her hard against the wall and carried them both over the edge with sharp, grinding jerks that actually felt as if the action might join them together.

A girl should be so lucky.

"Mmmm," she mumbled, plastering herself to him as he slipped out of her and lowered her feet to the floor.

"Pants off, then shower," he gasped, and she reluctantly unwound herself from his neck. He smelled like sunscreen —which he'd probably just worn for her because she was freaky about it—and sex and warm, yummy man beneath it all. It was an irresistible combination.

She leaned back against the door, watching as he shucked the rest of his clothes, then slid against his side when he held out his arm. "I'll have to go back on stage at the end, you know."

"And how much time do we have until then?"

"At least an hour."

He grinned down at her and squeezed her butt at the same time. "Perfect. Now let me tell me about my crazy plan to kidnap you to a hotel room tonight, and catch up with the tour buses tomorrow by helicopter..."

2

One good surprise deserved another. Mari grinned to herself as she climbed out of the airport limo—she was home, a day early because a planned stop in New York City for publicity had been bumped forward by a day, when she'd be en route to Wardham anyway. She was officially on break for her wedding and she couldn't wait to wrap her arms around her man and just relax for a night before the chaos descended.

Chase had mentioned he was going to his parents' for dinner, so she had the house to herself for at least an hour. She had every intention of surprising the hell out of her fiancé when he came home. She'd picked up a sexy bodysuit in Los Angeles that was seemed to be made of air and shadow. When the sales girl had pressed it into her hand, she'd laughed—the scrap of nylon looked like a swimsuit for a doll.

A very small doll.

But like a pair of stockings, it stretched. And stretched and stretched. Once she'd shimmied into it, she had to admit the knit pattern did fancy things to her curves. She looked exotic and alluring and perfect for a man who'd been deprived of physical affection for nearly three months, with a handful of too-brief exceptions.

He was going to rip this thing off of her in ten seconds, and it would still be worth it.

One of Chase's top priorities in having their home custom built was ensuring their privacy would be protected. There were skylights in almost every room, but no windows that couldn't be covered at the front of the house. So Mari didn't think twice about wearing the bodysuit and nothing else as she moved around the living room, lighting candles and setting the scene Chase would find when he got home. As soon as she heard his key in the lock, she scampered to the archway that separated the living room and the foyer, and struck what she hoped was a sexy pose.

All of her nerves jangled as she watched the handle turn. Was this ridiculous?

She closed her eyes as the door swung open—and waited.

When the reaction finally came—and it didn't take long, probably, but that stretch of silence still felt like ages —the laughing voice didn't belong to Chase.

"Nice outfit," said Audrey.

Which meant that Mari's friend and soon-to-be sister-in-law was standing fifteen feet away.

Mari wanted the ground to open up and swallow her whole. She squeezed her eyes shut. "Go away."

"I can see your...everything, pretty much. Just so you know." Audrey cleared her throat. "I guess I should turn around or something."

———

AUDREY WATCHED, totally amused, as her brother's fiancée sprinted past her and took the stairs two at a time, her body wrapped in not a lot of what could only be described as smoky grey dental floss. "It really is a nice outfit!"

"Shut up," Mari muttered not so quietly, her indignation floating down from the open balcony at the top of the foyer without any trouble. "What are you doing here?"

"Dropping off our dresses so they can hang in the spare room closet for a few days, de-wrinkle, that kind of thing. I tried to send them home with Chase, but he said he wanted to go sunset rock climbing with Evan instead."

"He's not on his way home?" Mari squeaked, popping back into view, now covered up with an oversized white robe.

Audrey burst out laughing. "No, he is. Sorry, that was mean."

Mari glared at her and stomped down the stairs. "Do you know how long it's been since I got laid last?"

"Off-limits conversation. Brother. Remember?"

"You don't care." Mari plopped down on the bottom step.

No, Audrey really didn't. But Chase would. He might be the oldest, but when it came to talking about sex, he was the most private. And when it came to Audrey, the baby, he preferred to think she was still ten years old.

Instead of answering, she did what she'd come over to do—hang up the dresses in the front closet, and then skedaddle so her brother and her best friend could have some much needed quality alone time. Which, as a secret grown-up, Audrey fully supported.

If the single men in her orbit weren't so completely awful, she wouldn't mind some quality alone time. Too bad her alone time of late was actually alone. And not particularly quality.

"I was kidding about Chase," she repeated once she turned back to her friend. "He should be here in ten minutes or so, he was just having a coffee with my dad when I left after dinner. But when I suggested he swing by my place and pick up the dresses, I thought his head might explode, so I decided to drive them over so they'd be waiting for you when you arrived...tomorrow."

Mari nodded, a pained expression written all over her face. It said, *"Uh-huh, that's nice, get out."*

Audrey could take a hint. She'd leave right after getting one last shot in because this was too funny. "And this way I got to see you for a minute. I just didn't realize I'd see that much of you."

"God." Mari buried her face in her hands. "You can put the dresses on the dining room table for now. I need to clear our winter stuff out of the closet to hang them up. And then you can get out of here before your brother gets back. Deal?"

She stalked over to her purse as Audrey did that, grabbing her phone before retreating to the steps. Surprising Chase had been a terrible idea. She was giving him a heads-up that she was home early.

CHASE BID his parents the world's fastest goodbye when he got Mari's message, but had to tamp down his teenage-boy libido when he saw his sister's compact SUV parked in front of his house five minutes later. He pulled past her and parked in the garage. The two-car deep, three-car garage was one of the few true excesses he'd allowed himself in building the new house. The last thing he wanted to do was stand out as a rich guy in a small town. On the other hand, his Porsche 911 needed a comfy home. So did his bike—especially his bike, since he wasn't driving it now— and his pickup truck, and Mari's car, which never got used these days. Add in a snow-blower and a riding lawn-mower, and the garage made all the sense in the world.

A justification he'd had to make to every single member of his family, bless their meddling hearts.

Speaking of meddling…

He shoved the door to the house open, bracing himself for yet another emergency wedding meeting with his darling baby sister, but while Audrey was waiting on the other side, it wasn't to pounce.

"Here he is!" she proclaimed loudly, amusement written all over her face. He looked "And I'm going to…go. Yes. Have a nice night, you two."

Did she wink at him as she squeezed under his arm and snuck out the door? Jesus Christ.

He turned the deadlock as soon as Audrey was on the other side of the door and turned his attention to his fiancée, huddled on the stairs in her bathrobe. "Hey, baby."

She made a face. "Hey."

"What's wrong?" He kicked off his shoes and sat next to her on the step. She leaned into his side and he kissed the top of her head before stroking his knuckle against her jaw, lifting her face to his. A second kiss—a real one this time —said everything he needed her to know. *I missed you. Welcome home.*

"I was waiting for you and Audrey came over instead and found me."

He laughed. "Sorry."

She pressed tighter against him, rubbing her face in his neck. "No, you don't understand. She *found* me."

"In our house? What a surprise."

"Naked."

Oh. Shit. He laughed again. "Totally, stark naked?"

She groaned. "No. Worse. I'm wearing a thing."

Hello. Now she had his full attention. "Show me."

"No!" She wailed the protest as she wrapped her arms around his waist. "I'm too embarrassed now. Also, I'm probably going to burn down the house, so can you go blow out all the candles in the living room?"

"Come on." Standing, he held out his hand. She stared at it for a minute, then took it with a sigh, shoving to her feet. "Don't be like that. At least it was Audrey and not my mother."

"Shut up, that's not funny." But she grinned. God, he loved her smile. Big and bright and it crinkled the corners of her eyes just so. "Okay, so if anyone was going to see me like that, Audrey was the best choice."

He pulled her close. "No, I'm the best choice."

The way her eyes softened? It did dangerous things to his heart. "That's what I meant."

"So I can see what's under this awful robe?"

"You bought me this robe." She gave him a mock shocked look.

"Ergo it's my property and I can burn it. Take it off."

She laughed and shook her head. "No way am I taking this off until we're safely in our bedroom. And then maybe the lights need to be turned way down."

"The lights are also my possession, and I decree, as lord and master of this manor, that they stay on." He swatted at her terry-cloth covered behind as she moved in front of him, leading the way into what did look like a nice, romantic setting in the living room.

But Chase didn't need candles or wine or soft lighting for a special night with Mari. He just needed her, soft and giving and not-stressed-out. He watched as she blew out the first candle, her eyebrows knitted tightly together in frustrated disappointment.

He took the opposite route around the room, helping her snuff out the flickering flames. At his twentieth candle, he straightened up and looked at her over his shoulder. "You've been back for what, an hour? Where did you get these candles?"

She stuck her tongue out at him. "Wedding supplies."

"So we were going to fuck in front of all these candles and then use them to decorate the reception?"

"Well, I hadn't thought about it like that." She shook her head and closed her eyes. "I'm terrible at this romantic surprise business."

He highly doubted that. If she had something on under that robe that she was embarrassed for his sister to see, that meant it was going to make his day. Week. He'd say month, but that included both their night together in Phoenix and their upcoming wedding, so it might be a stretch to assume, sight unseen.

With a single get-it-done breath he blew out the last five candles and picked up the chilling bottle of champagne. "Upstairs."

"I'm not sure I'm in the mood anymore," she pouted.

"Well, that's going to be super awkward when you take off that robe and I get the hard-on of the century." He crowded behind her and brushed his lips against the curve of her ear. "Why don't I show you what I've got on under my clothes first?"

That worked. She giggled and relaxed against his chest.

"Upstairs," he repeated, his voice lower and huskier than before. "And leave the robe down here."

3

Audrey shouldered open the door to Danny's, Wardham's only pub.

On the one hand, she shouldn't tell anyone about finding Mari all ready for sexy-times.

On the other, it was hilarious.

If Stella is here, you can share it with her. It seemed like a fair compromise.

Sadly, as she stepped into the bar, she only found Heath Edwards behind the bar and a few local guys she vaguely recognized but couldn't name at a table at the back. Heath was a great guy—one of her oldest friends, in fact—but not someone she could share her silly secret with.

"What can I get you, Audrey?"

Heath had been a good choice to replace Mari when she quit bartending. He had a way of leaning in and making eye contact with customers that made you want to sit down and unload your soul. And maybe your wallet, too.

Audrey thumped heavily on a stool at the bar and pointed at the row of bottles behind her friend's head. "Something with tequila and fruit juice."

"And ice, maybe? A margarita? With the good stuff, right?"

See? Good choice. She nodded, giving in to the up-sell. He was right. Burying a secret this hilarious would take the good stuff.

"How go the wedding plans?" he asked over his shoulder.

"Pretty good," she mumbled back as she rooted through the bowl of pretzels on the counter.

"Those are all pretty broken up," he said before turning on the blender.

She looked up. Wow. Not just good—he was an *excellent* bartender if he'd noticed she only ate whole pretzels. Heath. She crossed her arms and gave his back a solid once-over. What was his deal?

It had been years—no, decades—since she'd shared any secrets with him. In kindergarten, they'd fought over the green crayons, and in grade two, they'd started to hang out after school when their parents started to let them go biking up and down the street without close supervision. How many days had they paced back and forth in the empty lot that butted up against the ravine, talking about nothing and everything?

And then...she frowned. She didn't know what or when it had happened, but they'd faded into the kind of friends that always stopped and caught up at the drink table at a party and waved from across the street, but until he'd started working here, she couldn't say she'd exchanged more than a few sentences with him in ages.

They were the same age, twenty-three. He'd gone to university somewhere. Not Windsor, where she'd gone. Somewhere else. It niggled at the base of her neck that she didn't know.

She should know. She was a terrible friend if she didn't.

Staring at the back of his black t-shirt like it might give her some clues, she narrowed her eyes. Had he started working out? The t-shirt was faded and worn enough to not be a new purchase, but he'd never filled it out quite that much. He was *broad*.

Well, duh. He wasn't a teenage boy anymore.

Like maybe he could hear her thinking about him, he shot her a quick, curious look over his shoulder.

She shrugged.

He laughed under his breath and shook his head, his shaggy hair shaking like it was laughing at her too.

After pouring her drink in a salt-rimmed glass and sliding it across the bar at her, he crossed his arms—those had gotten bigger, too—and pinned her with an amused glance. "What's on your mind?"

"Nothing." She took a big, slurping swallow. "This is good."

"I know. I'm good."

"I was thinking that, earlier." She winked.

"About how good I am? I bet you were." He grabbed a bar towel from some magic hidden bartender space and slapped it on the counter next to her. "Can I get you a sandwich from the kitchen?"

She shook her head. "I ate at my parents. I'm good."

He laughed at the echo and she blushed.

"And I'm a linguist."

"I hear you actually are. Went to Japan for a year, eh?"

Oh, that. "I'm hardly fluent. I can order beer and grilled chicken and ask where the train station is."

"Still pretty cool. I'd love to hear more about—" He cut himself off as the door chimed and Sam Beadie walked in.

Eight years older than them, the oldest Beadie brother would normally be someone they only knew by name, but since Sam's little sister was marrying Audrey's oldest brother, they were practically family. And she had business with him.

"Hey," she called out, waving him over. "We need to talk about the bachelor party."

Sam gave her a slow eyebrow raise that said he wasn't sure they did. He was completely wrong. She pointed to the stool next to her, then turned back to Heath and swung her finger toward her delicious margarita. "Get him one of these."

"I'll have a draft lager, actually," he said, sitting down with a sigh. "Are you always this bossy?"

"Yes," said Heath as he pulled back the tap and poured Sam a beer.

"No." Audrey rolled her eyes. "I'm not being bossy. I just want to make sure we're all on the same page."

"Why? Are you coming to the bachelor party?"

She gave him a look.

"I've been talking to your brother about it. Don't worry."

Oh, that wasn't good. A man telling her not to worry almost guaranteed there was something that needed to be investigated there. "Don't let Davis talk you into clubbing. Chase will hate that."

Audrey was the youngest by a long shot, but that just meant that as long as she could remember, she'd been exposed to their much-older lives. Karen was thirteen years older than her, Chase ten years older, and even Davis, the closest in age, still had six years on her. So by the time she was six, Karen was off at college, Chase had been recruited into the OHL and was finishing high school while playing competitive hockey in Peterborough, and Davis had been the oldest kid at home.

And he'd been a hell-raiser.

Time hadn't changed that in the least.

Her world-traveling brother liked to work hard and

play harder, and on the rare occasion that he came home, he invariably tried to drag Chase out to have fun. When that failed, of late, he'd been taking Audrey. Unlike their older brother, Davis had no problem with Audrey being an adult now.

Plus she made a kick-ass wingman.

"Not Davis," Sam rolled his eyes. "We went to school together, remember? I know he's the best man, but since he doesn't get in until tomorrow, he's left the bachelor party to me. And Mari would kill me if it wasn't exactly what Chase wanted. Beer, poker, and a pay-per-view boxing match. I even rented those ridiculous poker tables."

She narrowed her eyes at him over her drink. "You don't sound thrilled. What would you rather be doing?"

He shrugged. "Doesn't matter. This hoopla makes my sister happy, that's all that matters."

"And you'd rather strippers or something?"

On the other side of the bar, Heath choked on a cough. Or a laugh, maybe. She shot him a look, too. Looks all round, that was the rule of the day, apparently. He cleared his throat when he realized she was seriously asking them that question. "Do you want him to answer?"

"Yes." She swivelled her head between the two men. "What?"

Sam sighed and rolled his eyes. "Audrey, it's a bachelor party. Other than the groom, who probably cares most about not pissing off his bride—and in this case, since that's my sister, I fully support that—yeah, the guys like strippers. Naked boobs are awesome. And don't give me that look. Seriously, you're scary good at that. You should be a kindergarten teacher or something. But you're not my mom or my sister or my girlfriend, so you get the cold hard truth. Boobs are awesome. Now drink your girly drink and shut up."

"You can't hire strippers for my brother's bachelor party."

He laughed. "I know. And I clearly can't tell you to shut up, either."

"This isn't a reassuring conversation," she muttered. On any level. She peeked at Heath, who'd busied himself with drying already dry glasses. "You agree with him?"

"About boobs being awesome? Yeah. Pretty sure that's true." He winked, but then put the glass down and crossed his arms again, suddenly serious. "I don't know about the rest. But I don't think Chase is the kind of guy to care one way or the other, and there's no doubt he only has eyes for Mari, so chill."

Chilling wasn't in Audrey's wheelhouse. "I'm going home," she announced, draining her glass. "Thank you, sir, for the drink." She nodded at Heath. "And you—" she stood and pointed at Sam. "If there are strippers, I will personally hold you responsible."

SAM WATCHED Heath watch Audrey head for the door, his eyebrows furrowed. "You worried about her driving?"

Heath shook his head and jerked his thumb over his shoulder. "Nah. She moved into Mari's old apartment when she moved back to town."

Two doors down.

"Ah." Sam should probably know that, but seriously, Audrey Miller was high-fucking-maintenance. The less he knew about her the better. She was best left to someone like Heath, who looked like he was more than up for the challenge.

"She's not—"

Sam lifted his hand and cut Heath off. "It's fine. And you know as well as I do that there aren't any strippers to hire around here. Not like that. We'd have to go into the city and nobody cares that much."

Heath nodded, granting him that truth.

One downside of living in the country, for sure—if you were a frat boy. Sam didn't care about strippers, that was for damn sure. He'd just said that to goad Audrey. He wasn't against them, per se, except for the unnecessary expense of hiring the fancy ones that would come to a bachelor party.

He couldn't get over the outlay already expected. Poker tables and catered sandwiches. Craft beer and single malt whiskey.

It wasn't that he begrudged his sister and her fiancé a

once-in-a-lifetime experience...except for the part where he thought that was all fucking ridiculous.

So maybe he did a little. They already were stupidly happy. And Chase didn't even like people, in general. Sure, he'd been pretty decent to Sam and his brothers and parents. He was a good guy, just not a social one.

Why the hell did he need a party thrown the night before the biggest party of his life?

If it were Sam getting married, he'd just want to lay low with his bride-to-be. Although given the fact that Wardham had zero single women that weren't related to him or best friends with his sister, the chances of him getting married were slim to none.

Plus nobody would want to marry a farmer who lived on a trailer at the back end of his parents' farm, anyway. The only thing he owned to his name was his truck. So instead of being the groom, he was the groomsman, and the host—at Evan West's house, because he didn't have a house of his own—of a bachelor party that he was pretty sure neither he nor the groom cared about attending.

"You look like you want another pint," Heath said from the far end of the bar, where he'd wandered when Sam drifted into his own head.

"Yeah. Thanks."

The younger man poured Sam his drink and then left him alone. Sam watched him unload the dishwasher and take another pitcher of beer to the guys in the back of the bar, then settle against the bar with a book.

He lifted his voice. "What are you reading?"

Heath looked up. "Studying, actually."

"Sorry." Sam returned his attention to his drink.

"No, it's fine." Heath moved closer and slid the book across the bar. *Regulatory Craft.*

"What the hell are you studying?"

Heath laughed. "Regulatory compliance. I'm thinking of starting my own business, providing assistance to companies too small to have their own in-house staff ensure they're compliant with different international standards."

"Shit, kid. That went in one ear and out the other. That's complicated stuff."

"Only when I use the unfamiliar terms. You know how you have information sheets that come with the supplies you need to use at the farm? Those are different around the globe. A local company who makes an organic feed supplement can't sell it in Mexico or Spain unless they provide all the regulatory data in Spanish—and that can all be outsourced, but how do they know if it's accurate? I can help with that."

Sam sat up a little straighter. "Again, I say shit. That sounds like a good idea."

Heath grinned. "I know."

"Might impress Audrey." The grin disappeared. Wrong thing to say, clearly, and it was none of his business. "Or anyone else. Everyone, probably. I'm sure there's nothing I can do to help, but if there is, you let me know."

Heath didn't answer immediately, but he didn't look away, either.

Moments like this, in Sam's experience, were what separated the boys from the men. Whatever it was, Heath had to want it enough to stake his claim to it. And if he didn't...

"Introduce me to Evan West," Heath blurted out, then stood up a little straighter. "Please. I have a whole business pitch. It's short and to the point—just enough to get me a meeting with him to present the whole plan. I can run it past you if you want."

Sam grinned. He liked this kid. "Not necessary. You want to come to a bachelor party on Friday night?"

4

———

Mari tried—and failed—not to glower at her fiancé as he pulled on a t-shirt, ignoring the fact that she was naked and on all fours on their bed.

"I won't be long," he promised.

"Lies." She flopped onto her belly and didn't move when he came over, which earned her a light swat on the bottom. "Don't do that if you don't mean it."

"We've spent the last day doing that and more," he teased before kissing the top of her head. "The county sports planning committee only meets once a month, on the second Friday. Which happens to be today. I don't want to miss the only meeting on my schedule for two weeks just because I'm getting married tomorrow. You could come with me."

She wrinkled her nose. She could. That would be reasonable. Or they could stay in bed, being filthy together, because she was apparently turning into a teenage boy or something. "No, go. I'll steam out the bridesmaid dresses and paint my nails."

He laughed. "You're going into the studio, aren't you?"

"Well if you're going to work, so am I."

"And that's why I love you."

He shifted, ready to move away from the bed, but she reached out and grabbed his hand. Scrambling back to her knees, she wrapped her arms around his neck. "I don't just want to you stay home so we can have sex, you know," she whispered in her ear. "I miss you all the time. And no matter how much I touch you now, I'm never going to get my fill of you."

Cupping her face, he kissed her softly, long enough to make her heartbeat pick up. "I'll be back in two hours. I promise."

She sighed as she thought about the schedule. "And then we have the rehearsal dinner and then we're going in two different directions for the night."

He winked at her. "But tomorrow I get to put a ring on it, right?"

"Don't say it like that." She stuck her tongue out at him. He stuck his right back, swiping the tips of their tongues together and making her dissolve into giggles. "Gross."

"Shush. Okay, an hour and a half. We can have a quiet snuggle before we head out for the rehearsal."

On that promise, Mari conceded they could be apart for a bit, and pulled on some workout clothes. Then she went to the kitchen and found a tub of cream cheese and a container of bell pepper and cucumber slices.

She'd already worked out plenty in the last thirty-six hours, and had the deliciously achy muscles to show for it.

As she headed toward the studio at the far end of the house, she heard a knock at the door. She kept going.

"Are you hiding somewhere?" Stella hollered after letting herself in.

Mari laughed and lifted her voice. "Studio!"

She put her snack on her desk and turned just as her best friend barrelled in and collided with her, wrapping her up in a big bear hug.

"I've missed you so much. And you've been home for two days and have done nothing but Chase."

Mari blushed. "Sorry. It's just..."

Stella waved off her excuses. She got it. They'd been best friends since forever and didn't need to be the first visit or anything. That's why they were besties. "Besides— tonight is going to be amazing. Everyone is coming to Audrey's apartment for your bachelorette party, and we'll get lots of time to talk then."

Audrey was living in Mari's old place, and while it was small, it was also cool by Wardham standards—cute and funky by more urban metrics—and close enough for everyone in town to walk.

"And it's not like we don't talk constantly," she contin-ued, moving around the desk to grab a clipboard off a hook on the wall. In the last three months, Stella had slipped into the role of Mari's...something. Assistant sounded weird. Right-hand woman, maybe. It had started when Mari's phone had fritzed at the same time as her laptop accidentally went to the wrong city and she hadn't been able to post to social media for a few days. In a panic, she'd called Stella and in a few short minutes, she had her calmed down and the situation under control.

It turned out that her best friend was a good person to mimic her online personality, because she paid attention to everything Mari posted. Knew that she did a giveaway on Thursdays that stretched over the weekend and Mondays were for music she liked. Even knew what kind of pictures to put up on Instagram and how often tweets should be going out—and who to tag in them.

Stella was a quiet workhorse, and since that panicky call, had been doing most of Mari's social media stuff. It only took her a few hours a week, so Mari could afford to pay her a reasonable wage, too—despite Chase's wealth, she was committed to doing the music thing as much on her own two feet as she could. And that definitely stretched to hiring staff.

Especially staff who were likely to gossip on the job— something Mari strongly encouraged, of course.

"Have you and Chase talked about what what wedding pictures will be circulated? And how?"

Mari wrinkled her nose. "No. He keeps changing the subject when I bring it up." Which she'd only done twice, because it felt like a conversation that would never get anywhere. Her fiancé was a stubborn butt when it came to privacy—a fact she appreciated, but it made it an extra challenge to build an online platform. She knew he wanted to wait to release a formal wedding photo once it was safely in the past, but that wasn't how the internet worked.

"Well, I have some ideas." Stella pulled her cell phone from her back pocket, typed in her password, and handed it over. "Here are some wedding announcements on Instagram that capture moments without actually showing very much. Do you think he'd be okay with something like that?"

On the screen were a series of pictures that looked like a magazine spread of an intimate, romantic wedding—all without showing anyone's face or location details. Mari grinned. "I love these. Yes, something like this would be perfect. A lot of these, actually—maybe four or five, over the course of the day?"

"Got it." Stella took her phone back and pursed her lips. Aha. The gossip tangent. Mari laughed before her friend even said anything. "What? I didn't say it?"

"You don't need to. Yes, tell Audrey about the plan so she can check it off her list and put it in her binder."

"Has she been super annoying this week?" Stella made a face. "I'll admit, I love her to death, but if I ever get married I'm eloping. She can't help herself with the planning takeover."

"Actually, I appreciate it. I do! Look at what you're

doing for me. I can't handle Facebook and Twitter, I can't be left in charge of a wedding. And then with the tour coming up...she's been a godsend. A bossy godsend, but still."

"Good good. What else should we talk about before I leave you to it?"

Mari filled her in on a potential Australia-Asia tour that would cover a good chunk of the winter, and how anxious she was to get back into the studio and record a full-length album. "It's hard to choose, you know? Like it feels like these tours are a once-in-a-lifetime opportunity, and I don't want to say no to anything, but I also want—no, need—to come home for more than a week. To work, but also to spend time with Chase. And you guys, too. Of course."

Stella blew a raspberry at her. "We will always be here. Except for Audrey, of course, who might go bounding off on another adventure somewhere. But then she'll come back, too."

"I love you, Stell. So much. This whole wedding thing is making me hardcore nostalgic and weepy, so brace yourself for more of that at the end of the night, okay?"

"Sure thing. One of the best things about weddings is all the feels." Stella beamed for a second, then looked down at her clipboard. "For the two days after the wedding, when you guys are in Banff before rejoining the tour, you want radio silence online, yes?"

And just like that, they slipped back into work mode.

———

SAM HAD NEVER BEEN SO glad to hang out with a bunch of dudes—and only dudes. For a guy that lived alone in a trailer, he'd been surrounded for what felt like days by women who alternated in a random, unpredictable pattern between over-the-top giddiness and bizarre weeping. The feelings that weddings seemed to bring out in people were unreal.

Evan was on the phone when Sam arrived, but he waved him in and pointed to the open-concept kitchen that looked like it had never been used. Two wait staff were setting up the catering for the night. Sam stood there, suddenly unsure of himself—he'd never done this before.

Luckily the staff had. "Are you Mr. Beadie?" one of them asked.

"Yeah." He shoved his hands in his pockets. "This looks great. Thank you. Should I settle up with you now?"

"Mr. West took care of the balance owing." She smiled at him like that made all the sense in the world.

Sam's face burned up. It only made sense if everyone had already accepted that it was better if Sam didn't foot the bill.

Damnit. He was no charity case. He'd agreed to have the bachelor party here because it made sense, but...ah hell. It wasn't like any part of this had been within his control, not really. He scrubbed his hand over his face and pulled out his wallet. Extracting two fifty-dollar bills, he folded them individually and handed them to the servers. "Well, thank you again, then. This is an extra something for the help tonight."

After they took their tip, he left them to their work and went to find Evan to have an awkward conversation about money, but the man had disappeared somewhere. And then the doorbell chimed.

On the other side stood the official best man of the wedding, and possibly the only person in the entire spectacle that Sam actually knew well—they'd only been a year apart at school and played hockey together for years. His face cracked into a relieved smile and he held out his hand. "Davis, you jerk, nice to see you show up at last."

Chase Miller's world-traveling brother stepped into the house, grasping Sam's hand and pulling him in for a one-armed man-hug. "Fuck you, too, man. How's it going?"

"Yeah. Good." Sam glanced over Davis's shoulder. "Looks like people are starting to show up."

Three more cars pulled in, joining the two that had already parked. Men he didn't recognize spilled out of them all.

"Shall we get this circus underway?" Davis asked, slinging his arm around Sam's neck as he spun around so they stood shoulder to shoulder, ready to greet the guests. "It's going to be good."

It proved to be something, that was for sure.

Good at times—Chase's friends liked poker and weren't particularly skilled at it, so Sam found himself up a few hundred by the time the pay-per-view boxing match started. And before too long, his brothers arrived, along with Ian Nixon and Paul Reynolds, two more local men. The balance was shifting again, and the tightness in Sam's chest eased.

But while most of the hockey guys seemed decent enough, one asshole kept rubbing him the wrong way. At first he couldn't figure out what Zach Brenton was doing that pushed his buttons—he was just joking around and playing cards like everyone else. But he had this hard edge to him, and by the fourth negative retort, Sam realized the NHL forward literally had nothing good to say. And he was argumentative as fuck.

"Come on, Manny!" Chase yelled at the television, urging his favourite boxer to get his head in the match.

"This is gay," Brenton muttered.

Whoa. Sam snapped a look at Chase, then Evan. Neither of them said anything. What the hell?

It's not like he went out of his way to be an ally or whatever Mari called it, but that was childish, off-side name calling at any time. And maybe the guy didn't know that Evan was gay, but still, he was a fucking grown up and should act like one.

Plus he was a dick. Which made Sam want to stomp on him and take some of the overhyped swagger out of his step.

Picking a fight the night before the wedding probably was a bad idea.

"Hey, man," he said, keeping his voice low. "Choose a different word, eh?"

"Eh." Brenton snickered. "Canadian homeboy gonna tell me how to talk?"

"If you need a lesson, absolutely." Sam shoved to his feet a split second after Brenton. The ass wanted to get in his face? Fine. Zach might work out with fancy trainers and throw down his stick from time to time, but Sam did real man's work from sun up to sun down. He didn't need weights or a gym, although every time he stepped in one he had no problem keeping up with his friends.

If Brenton wanted Sam to demonstrate his ability to bench press Zach's dumb-ass self through Evan's window, Sam would happily oblige.

"Break it up," Davis said, shouldering between them. "The fight's on TV and that's where it's going to stay. Come on." He thumped Sam on the chest and shoved him toward the back door, grabbing two beers on his way.

That would have been the end of it if Brenton had just sat down. But Chase was on his feet now, looking at them both in confusion, and apparently the other man didn't have enough grace to just fucking say sorry.

"You've got some rude friends, Miller."

Sam surged against Davis's arm. He wanted rude?

Chase held up his hands, one palm pointing at Sam and the other at his former teammate. "What are you guys doing?"

"That fag—"

Sam wasn't sure who hit Brenton first, Evan or Chase, but they both went for him. Damnit, he wanted to be the one with the bruised knuckles. The girls would lecture the hell out of him if it was Chase.

He, on the other hand, would buy his brother-in-law all the ice he needed. He rocked back on his heels and watched with undisguised delight as Chase hauled Brenton back to his feet.

"One chance to say you're sorry, Zach," the groom ground out, clearly no longer in the mood to play peacemaker. "That kind of language isn't on here."

"Sure. Sorry." The worst apology ever. Brenton shrugged his shoulders back like he was shaking off a bad play instead of blatant hatred. "Too much testosterone. You know what? We should get some chicks here."

"Why, because a guy's night threatens your sexuality?" Sam shook his head after sniping that across the room. Unreal.

Brenton sneered at him. Could the guy be any more of a stereotypical douchebag? Why the hell did Chase invite him in the first place?

"You want to send a car over to the inn to get your date, Zach? I don't have a problem with that." Chase had slipped on an easy half-smile, but there was an edge to his voice that said he wouldn't be pushed.

Like there was a history here or something that Sam wasn't privy to.

The two hockey players stared each other down, and it

was Brenton that looked away first. "Nah. More poker, maybe."

Chase clapped him on the shoulder. "Good deal." He turned to Evan. "Sorry about that."

Their host gave a brusque nod, and that was all Sam saw before Davis propelled him outside.

Sam waited until the patio doors closed behind them to let loose. And his friend let him fly with his rant, but when he stopped, Davis didn't hold back his advice to chill out.

"You're not going to change his mind, and tonight isn't really the time or place."

"Fuck that, man. I don't care about changing his mind. I'm not an activist or something. But he's an asshole. I shouldn't have to put up with that just because he's some rich hockey player."

"Are you gay?" Davis squinted. "That might have come out wrong. I mean, cool if you are, and it's not of my business. I'm just saying, why is this your fight all of a sudden?"

"I think it's more about being a decent human being," Sam muttered, because fuck no he wasn't gay, but that wasn't the point.

"You've been on edge since I got here. You sure him being an idiot wasn't just an excuse to blow up at someone?"

An instant rebuttal itched on the tip of his tongue, but it tasted like a lie. And given what he'd just said about being decent... He took a pull from his beer instead.

Davis, also decent, didn't say anything else. Point made, point taken.

The door slid open as they were nearing the bottom of their bottles. Chase joined them, and he brought replacement beverages. "Cheers, my brothers." He grinned. "I already did this with Gavin and Travis inside. To your gorgeous sister, Sam. I'm marrying her and gaining enough forwards to make my own shinny team."

Sam laughed. "Ready to get back on the ice, then?"

Chase shrugged. "Maybe this winter. Don't tell my dad in case I change my mind. Mari's tour schedule is a factor, too. Did she tell you she's been offered a spot on a tour to Australia?"

No.

Sam was pretty sure his parents didn't know that, either. "Australia, eh?"

He ignored the look Davis shot him. Okay, maybe he had some issues to work through. Didn't change the fact that Brenton was an asshole. Or that his little sister was on the cusp of serious stardom.

Shit. He tipped back his beer and reminded himself the latter was a good thing.

The door slid open again, and Evan West, Wardham's original man of mystery, stepped outside...trailed by Heath Edwards. "Sam?"

Fuck. "Hey, Heath, you made it. Evan, this is Heath."

Their host gave him an amused look. "Yes. We've met at Danny's many times."

"Right. Of course." Sam needed another drink. And like forty-eight hours alone in his trailer where he could watch Netflix and read books and not have to interact with the outside world. Sam and other people were not a good combination right now. And that had to wait until after the weekend, so he took a deep breath and manned up. "But I asked Heath to come here tonight to talk to you, actually, if you've got a few minutes…"

5

Mari woke up on the morning of her wedding day, no surprise, to Audrey's gleeful face.

"Morning," her friend whispered, her eyes sparkling like she was already halfway through her to-do list for the day. "I brought you coffee, and we've got mimosas and some fruit and croissants downstairs."

"Uhmmm...." Mari swallowed hard, trying to get rid of her cottonmouth. "Okay."

"You've got lots of time for breakfast and a shower. The stylists are set to arrive in forty-five minutes. Stella's here already, Karen's on her way over, and I just texted your mom to let her know you were getting up. I'm sure she'll be here soon."

"You and my mom are texting?" Mari shoved the bedding aside and padded across the room to the master bath. She trusted that Audrey would follow. She wasn't wrong.

"Of course. That's how today is going to run like clockwork. Everyone has everyone else's number. Except for you. No phone for you today."

"Just a strict timeline and orders?"

"In you go," Audrey instructed, reaching past her to turn on the shower.

"I can do that myself."

"You weren't."

Mari gave her friend an amused, half-awake smile. "I was waiting for you to leave the room so I could pee first."

"Oh."

"Yeah."

"I'll be downstairs."

"Great."

Fifteen minutes later, Mari found not only her new sisters-in-law and her best friend in her kitchen, but also her mother and Chase's mother and a hairdresser and makeup artist that looked like they burst out of the same morning-people pod that Audrey was formed in.

"There's the bride!" her mother exclaimed, swooping in for an emotional hug.

"Yep, here I am." She pressed her hand to her fluttery belly. "Where's the wine?"

"It's seven-thirty in the morning, dear." Her mother nodded quickly when Mari gave her an *are you kidding me* look. "Right. It's on the breakfast bar. Audrey's thought of everything, hasn't she?"

Mari gave her mom a kiss on the cheek. "She really has. I didn't even know you knew how to text. You don't text me!"

"Well, I will now that Audrey's shown me how these app things work on my phone. Can I get you some breakfast?"

"I'd kill someone for a waffle. We probably have pancake mix in the cupboard."

Her mother squeezed her hand. "I'm on it."

"Dad coming over later?"

"He said to call him as soon as you're done the getting in the dress in your lacy underthings photographs."

"Mom!" Mari blushed. Of course her dad wouldn't even want to be in the house when there was talk of blue garters and squealing over the corset she'd squeeze into under her strapless dress. That didn't need to be spelled out.

"Oh sweetie." Her mother winked. "Maybe you should have some of that wine after all."

No kidding.

She kept it to a single glass of bubbly though, letting Audrey top it up with orange juice every so often, and by the time her hair and make-up were done, and the photographer had captured both her dress hanging in the bedroom window and the risqué corset back as she stepped into the dress, helped by Stella, Karen and Audrey, she was more than ready to have a moment with her dad. Sweet, chaste, *real*. Her father was her anchor, and she needed him.

"Can you call him now?" she asked her mom.

"Sure. Why don't you girls head downstairs?"

Mari had never thought of her parents as being playful. Maybe her mother had been, once upon a time, before she'd been abandoned, pregnant with twins with two crazy-ass young sons hanging off either leg.

That kind of fucked-up bullshit would knock the playful out of anyone.

Even after Mark Beadie quietly staked his claim and moved onto the farm, marrying Fern and adopting her young children, there remained a permanent undercurrent of responsibility. Mari couldn't begrudge her parents that motivation to work hard and provide for their family —she'd learned through their example the value of digging in and doing the grunt work that got you ahead.

So when her mother waved her off, refusing to let too many tears fall in front of her daughter on her wedding day, Mari took that at face value. She left her mom in the master bedroom and lifted her dress, carefully stepping onto the staircase that descended into the foyer.

And that's when her dad walked in the front door.

"Oh my god," Mari cried out, the tears already sliding down her face. "You were waiting?"

He laughed and wiped his own suspiciously wet eyes. "I wouldn't miss this for the world."

"Mom said you were at home..." she warbled. "And now my makeup is going to need to be re-done."

"Worth it," he said, smiling broadly. "You are the most beautiful bride I have laid eyes on since your mother married me. Come here and give your old man a hug."

She carefully picked her way down the stairs, then flew into his arms. Screw propriety and stoicism. "I love you, Daddy. So much."

"Same, my ladybug. I'm so proud of you. And that fellow you're marrying isn't so bad."

She grinned and pressed her wet face tighter against his neck. "He has all the respect in the world for you."

"As he should. I'm his elder."

Now she was shaking with giggles. "Okay."

"Pull yourself together, now. Your brothers aren't far behind me." Translation: emotional moment was over because no way was he setting that example for his sons.

Mari stifled an eye roll and tucked her arm through his, leading him into the kitchen where the makeup artist immediately descended and started the repair job.

The morning started to speed up from that point. All three brothers arrived together. Travis and Sam were tight-lipped about the night before, but Gavin opened up as soon as they had a minute alone. The twin connection trumped any brother code.

"Chase said that Sam got into it with one of the Coyotes last night," she whispered as they were shifted into position by the photographer for a formal picture.

Gavin laughed. "Yeah, I thought Sam was going to take his head off."

"Gav! Don't encourage him like that."

"Nah, he was fine. And in the right, actually."

"I know. I just worry about him sometimes." She flicked her gaze toward her oldest brother, who was leaning against the deck railing and staring out onto the lake. "He's not happy."

"It's a wedding, Mar. None of us are happy."

She elbowed him in his side. "You know what I mean."

"I do. And today isn't the day to worry about that. Got it?"

Nope. She didn't get it in the least. "I'm going to talk to him."

"I'm standing on your train, so you're going to stay right where you are and smile for the camera." Gavin slid his arm under her hair and veil and slung it over her shoulder.

"Perfect!" called out the photographer.

Hardly, thought Mari. She was only home for a few days. So what if it was her wedding? Didn't that mean she could talk about whatever she wanted and her brothers would have to like it? Or at the very least, put up with it?

Next up was the entire family, with her parents on either side of her and her brothers fanning out around them. Then all the kids, and as soon as the photographer said they were done and Audrey pronounced she had almost two hours to chill before the ceremony—because reasons Mari didn't really get, but also didn't care about, as she loved her dress and sitting quietly with her best friends and family sounded like the perfect preamble to a crazy, whirlwind afternoon.

The photographer departed first, then the make-up artist gave Stella and Audrey an SOS kit in case Mari started crying again.

And finally her house was quiet again.

"More wine, honey?" her mother asked.

"Maybe half a glass." She scrunched her nose at her father's raised eyebrow. "It's a special occasion."

"You used to say that about pop, too," he said. "Until you got a cavity and we had to go to the dentist for a filling."

"I don't think champagne will give me a cavity," she giggled.

"Still. Can't be healthy." He winked, taking the edge off his lecture.

Stella, ever the eager conversationalist, leaned in and asked Mari's dad what he'd prefer to toast with at dinner if he didn't like to drink alcohol, and that sent Audrey scurrying for her binder.

Travis and Gavin followed their mother into the kitchen for drinks, and Mari saw her opening to talk with Sam.

He saw it too, and stood up. "I'm going to head to the winery now, I think."

She narrowed her eyes at him. Well, she'd bought a

comfortable dress she could easily move in for a reason. Leaping to her feet, she said, "I'll walk you out, then."

Waiting until the front door was closed behind them and they were alone in the front drive—except for the security guard at the road, but he couldn't care less about Mari talking to her brother. He was just watching for paparazzi.

Sam followed her gaze. "That's something, eh?"

"Don't worry about it," she said, pressing her hand to his forearm. "You good?"

"I think that's my question for you, little sister."

"I'm not the one picking fights and being all squirrelly. What's going on?"

"Nothing."

She glared at him. "Do I look stupid?"

"No, you look like a pampered beauty queen in a dress that cost as much as my truck." Mari gasped and stepped back and Sam's face fell as he realized how that sounded. "Shit—"

"This dress cost me like, five hundred dollars off the rack, you asshole!" Name calling was probably offside, but so was him projecting whatever his issues were onto her. Gavin had been right. This wasn't the conversation to be having today of all days. "You know what? I was just worried about you, but if you want to be like that—"

They were talking over each other now, a jumble of offended sensibilities and half-apologies. "Forget I said that, okay?"

"How can I forget it? You *just* said it."

"Water under the bridge."

She grunted a displeased huff. "I don't think that means what you think it does."

"Well, you're the fancy songwriter, so you'd know."

Fuck. She swallowed the rude response that she wanted to jam down his throat. It was so easy to be mean to each other. The cruel price to pay for having siblings—the best of friends and the worst of enemies. She didn't want any of her brothers to be an enemy today. Not even someone who was clearly spoiling for a fight. "Sam…"

He walked a few paces away, then turned and gave her a lopsided grin that didn't get anywhere near his eyes. "You look beautiful, Mari. Chase is a lucky man."

Her heart cracked and she pressed her hand to her chest. "I'm a lucky sister. Never forget that, okay?"

He nodded and she watched him turn and walk to his truck. He didn't spray gravel or spin out of the drive onto the road at unnecessary speed, but there was still an urgency to his departure that told Mari it wasn't forgotten or water under the bridge.

Shit was right.

———

SAM KNEW he was acting unconscionably—he owed Mari a huge apology, but every time he opened his mouth, something else came out.

So much for being a decent guy. He was a selfish, angry man who couldn't see past the end of his own nose. He needed to shake it off and just be happy for his baby sister on her wedding day.

Pretend to fit in. How hard could that be?

For a guy driving a beat-up pickup truck that no car wash could get entirely clean, pretty damn hard. He'd gotten the inside professionally detailed this week, but he'd still needed to haul some hay the day before, and... well, there was no way around the fact that he was a country hick who had recently developed an impulse-control problem.

Being dressed in a suit that cost more than his last feed bill didn't change the fact that he had no clue how to wear it—or play the games it seemed to call for.

His shoulders hitched up as he took the hill out of town. In the last few years, the stretch between Wardham and Kingsville had gotten downright fancy—and Go West Winery led the charge in that respect.

The winery sat at the end of a long, tree-lined drive, right on the edge of the lake. The modern glass building to the right housed the vineyard operations, the banquet hall, the wine shop, and the various offices. On the far side of the parking lot was the all-that-is-old-is-new-again orig-inal mansion that had recently been turned into a modern, luxurious inn.

Of course it had.

Because nothing about Wardham could stay sleepy and faded and normal.

Sam gritted his teeth together as he walked across the parking lot and pulled open the door to the main winery building. The spacious lobby was empty, but he could hear staff moving around in the banquet hall. The ceremony would be outside, on the back terrace overlooking the lake, before moving inside for cocktails and dinner and dancing.

He'd been to a few nice weddings in the last couple of years—many of them in this very same building. The West brothers certainly knew how to throw a party.

But the Millers had gone all out. It definitely wasn't the Beadies who'd picked trees draped in pearls for the extravagant centrepieces, that was for damn sure. For every time he and his father disagreed on something, they *never* wasted money like that.

"You look like you just swallowed something sour," a gentle voice sounded from the staircase.

Sam turned his head to the side, then rocked back on his heel. Well, damn. Big eyes, shiny golden brown hair, and curves that filled out a bright red dress like magic. He grinned at the beautiful woman who now stood where a moment before there had been nobody. "Sorry about that," he murmured, moving closer to the perfect excuse to get out of his head. "I thought I was alone with my thoughts."

Her eyes twinkled. "So you don't deny the thoughts were sour. Are you a jilted lover or something?"

He laughed. "Grumpy older brother, actually. To the bride."

"Oh." She gave a knowing smile. "Marrying into the NHL world can be a bit overwhelming."

Hardly. He knit his eyebrows together. "My sister's on tour with Alaskan Nights right now. I don't think a bunch of hockey players could overwhelm her."

The redhead wrinkled her nose. "Sorry. I may have been projecting."

Don't get involved, don't get involved... "You're here with one of the players?"

"Sort of." She shrugged. "I mean, yes. But we're just friends. Not that it matters." She blushed. "Anyway, we were told we could explore the winery. That's what I was doing."

"Exploring sounds like fun. Did you see everything you were looking for?" Sam knew he should get the box of programs and mill around the entrance to greet any other early arrivals—that would be appropriate penance for being a dick—but there was something about this woman...like maybe she didn't quite fit in, either. "I could give you a more thorough tour."

Like hell he could. He'd only been here for weddings, didn't know the first thing about wine, and there was a solid chance that any commentary he had to offer would be heavily slanted toward rich people being out-of-touch snobs. No matter how cute this woman was, he needed to walk away. Go find some duct tape and cover his mouth before he inadvertently offended his sister's guest.

"Really?" The woman took the last two steps down the staircase and held out her hand. "I'm Gillian. And I'm definitely interested in a thorough tour—of whatever you want to show me."

———

CHASE PACED AHEAD of his brother toward the winery. They killed a good amount of time his parents' house, but since his sisters were with Mari, there weren't many family pictures that could be taken—except a few with his six month old nephew, little Will. His parents had gleefully signed up for baby duty while his brother-in-law ran wedding morning errands and Karen did the bridesmaid thing. Even on his wedding day, Chase was no longer the most important boy in his parents' life.

He couldn't blame them. He'd had a good run. Thirty-three years was probably a solid fifteen years too long, anyway—a point Davis had laughingly made on the drive over.

And right now his brother was trailing behind him, muttering something about a groom stepping back and letting other people handle shit, today of all days.

Chase threw a good-natured, nothing-can-ruin-this-day grin over his shoulder. "Shut up, it's not like I have anything else to do. Might as well get here early to greet guests."

Davis smoothed out his jacket and tugged on his cuffs. For a man who lived in board shorts and sunscreen-stained tank tops, he had a secret GQ side that Chase hadn't expected. "I think Mari's brothers are doing that."

Chase spun around in a slow circle, his open palms sweeping the empty space around them. "Obviously not."

"That's Sam's truck over there," Davis pointed out.

"Maybe he dropped it off and ran an errand. Maybe he went to find Brenton to throw-down again. I don't know." Chase wiped his hands on his pants. "Who thought it was a good idea to have the ceremony in the afternoon? That's a hell of a lot of waiting around time."

Davis laughed. "Seems kind of standard with weddings, dude."

Dude. There was his brother. Chase had started to worry for a minute. He grinned. "We should go inside and find a drink."

Davis winked. "No need to look anywhere else." He pulled a thin flask from his breast pocket and handed it over. "I've got you covered."

As soon as he twisted off the cap, Chase caught a whiff of grassy rye. Full-proof, straight up. "Were you planning on getting us drunk?"

"Just a nip." Davis winked and took the flask after Chase tipped back a shot. "And enough for Sam, Gavin, and Travis if—I mean when—they show up."

"When, you dickhead. We're early. They're not late."

Davis took another shot and fixed his gaze on Chase's neck. "Come here."

"What?" Chase hopped backwards, batting his brother's hand out of the way. "Leave my tie alone."

"I'm just fixing it."

"Fuck off. It's fine. Let's go check out the set-up inside. Maybe find a bridesmaid for you to hit on or something."

"Now you're talking." Davis perked up, but just for a second. "Hey, I'm related to all the bridesmaids."

"Not Stella."

"Practically."

Chase shrugged. "Sorry."

"No you're not. You don't care about the plight of the single man."

He grinned. Nope. Not his problem anymore—or ever again.

———

It took Gavin exactly three seconds to figure out that Mari had done exactly what he'd warned her not to do.

"Don't give me that look," she said, setting down the glass of orange juice she'd just shot back, wishing it was wine.

"It's your wedding day. Why did you have to poke the bear?"

"I couldn't help myself, clearly."

"You okay?"

She let out a wry laugh. "That's what I asked him. Apparently a land mine of a question."

"It's hard for him," Gavin said, lowering his voice. "Seeing you move into a different life. Be away."

"I'm not like...*him*." They both knew she was referring to their birth father—a man neither of them had ever met, but Sam and Travis remembered.

"I know that. And Sam knows that, too."

"He can't put that on me, though."

"Is he? Or is he trying to just deal with his shit, all by himself?"

And she'd pushed Sam to talk when he didn't want to. Damn. "Right." Tears welled up again and she closed her eyelids, refusing to let them fall. "Why are weddings so stressful?"

"No clue. Take a deep breath, let it out, and promise me you're not going to try to fix Sam's fucked up head again today." She scrunched up her face and he laughed. "Okay. Whatever. Just...your guy can throw a wicked right hook, so don't get into it with Sam again in front of Chase."

6

———

"So this is the back hallway," Sam said slowly, his words trailing off as Gillian swayed toward him. The ridiculousness of what he was saying pushed against him for a second, but then she laughed, and it lit up her eyes.

"Fascinating," she whispered. He dropped his gaze to her mouth—plump, shiny with lip gloss he wanted to nibble away.

Like he had a shot with a woman like this.

A woman who was here with someone else. *Just a friend*. Did that matter?

Sam was a traditional guy. Yeah, it should matter.

But Gillian *sparkled*. From the inside out, and something about her grabbed at his guts and hung on for dear life. If she gave him a clear invitation, he was going to take it. Damn the consequences.

She'd patiently followed him through the great hall and across the terrace—both of which looked perfect and ready for the wedding of the century to happen in a little less than two hours. Now they were were in, as he'd already explained, the back hallway that ran beneath the suite of offices upstairs.

Any second, no matter how slowly they walked, they'd be back in the great hall. He'd go and loiter in the lobby until guests started to arrive, and she'd head back to her room.

"So, I've shown you around..." He stepped away from her, but only to give himself enough room to turn towards her and run the pads of his fingers along the sweet curve of her arm without being creepy. Leaning against the wall, he touched her just enough to invite her to move in closer. A suggestion, no pressure. Hopefully not too much of a plea, but God, she smelled good and felt better, and he wanted the world to stop so this moment could stretch on forever. When was the last time he'd been able to lose himself in a big pair of eyes? "But I haven't asked you anything about yourself."

She did him one better than just take the invitation to stop and talk. She closed the gap between them to a scant inch and danced her index finger up the squiggly pattern on his tie. He'd taken off his jacket in the great hall, hanging it over his chair at the head table. Gillian had taken a few opportunities before to touch his arm as they walked and talked, but now she was right in front of him, and the touch was anything but accidental.

Almost definitely on purpose, her pinky finger trailed to the side, sliding up the front of his shirt, and he gave silent thanks for his sister not wanting them in a traditional tux with a vest. On the other side of his thin dress shirt, his muscles pulsed against her touch. Eager for more of it and willing to do just about anything to get it.

"What do you want to know?" Her breath puffed warm and sweet between them as she whispered the question, looking at his tie as she asked it. Then she blinked up at him and it took all of his willpower not to haul her tight against him. Get rid of that inch of space and consume her like she'd already somehow consumed him.

He cleared his throat and let his hands settle lightly on her waist—not that it made a difference to how his body reacted. His pulse picked up and he desperately wanted to dip his head and taste of her lips. He settled for more conversation, which with Gillian wasn't exactly a hardship. "Where are you from?"

"Vermont, originally. Arizona for the last three years."

"No more snow for you."

"I like the snow, actually." She floated her hips left, then right, beneath his hands, and his cock lifted toward her and his balls drew tight. "Skiing, snowboarding... snowball fights."

"You would be a very distracting opponent, I'm sure."

"I'd go easy on you."

"No you wouldn't."

She laughed and pressed in close, her belly brushing his erection. "No. I wouldn't."

Holding his breath, he froze. She didn't pull away. His dick flexed toward her and he couldn't summon any shame, even though this was wrong.

"I should let you get back to your date," he said gruffly, his hands flexing on her hips.

"Zach Brenton is face down in his pillow right now, and even if he wasn't, I don't want to spend any time alone with him. I'd say coming with him on this trip was a mistake, except I quite like this town. And right now, I quite like you, too."

"Brenton is your date?" Fuck propriety. Fuck the rules. That ass-wipe didn't deserve this woman, and she deserved more than to be rejected twice in a weekend. Skating one palm up her side, he found her hand and tangled their fingers together. "I'm sorry about that. Maybe I can make it up to you."

"How so?" Her eyes danced as he brought her knuckles to his lips. Why she was thrilled, he couldn't quite figure out—his skin didn't feel like silk or smell like candy. But if she was game, he'd make the next hour good for her.

Way better than Brenton ever could.

"The tour isn't over yet," he murmured, sliding his other hand into the small of her back as he moved his lips from her hand to her mouth. She parted her lips immediately, and the touch of her tongue against his was like a spark to the dry kindling that was his resolve to not go too far.

Fuck that.

They were going as far as they possibly could. He pressed deeper, swallowing her sounds of pleasure and pleas for more. Oh, he'd give her more. He'd give her everything he had.

He glanced up and down the hall, then spun them around, holding her tight as he tried the nearest door.

A storage closet. It would do.

"See?" he said once they were inside and he had her pressed into a body-shaped space between the door and the first shelf. "The tour continues."

"Wow." Her voice hitched as he trailed his hand down her hip. Over her thigh. Fuck....

Every time he touched a bit more of her bare skin, he thought it was the best thing he'd ever felt. Her thigh was smooth skin and firm muscle, with a soft promise of pillowy goodness at the top. And she was wearing stockings, completely with the little ribbons attached to something that felt like it was made of satin and sin. "This," he said roughly, "is the debauching closet."

Her lips quirked as she fluttered her eyelashes up at him. "Is that so? I hear they're very rare. What a lucky find."

"Today I think I'm the luckiest man in town," he

murmured, lowering his mouth to hers. "Maybe the entire country..."

He kissed her as his questing fingers explored the entire fascinating geography beneath her skirt—the edge of her stockings, the sweet skin above them, and the curve of her hip and the lush sweep of her ass.

And then finally, when he'd touched her everywhere else and couldn't wait another minute more, and she gave him the breathiest, sexiest *yes* he'd ever heard, he slid his hand between her legs and cupped her sex.

"Ohhhh, Sam." Gillian's cheeks were pink and her lips were still wet from his mouth as she tipped her head back against the wall and fixed her half-mast gaze on his face. She looked so good it should be illegal. He rocked his palm more firmly over that thin strip of lace separating him from her pussy.

"You feel amazing on my hand." He nipped at her lower lip. "Tell me I can touch you. Tell me I'm going to get to find out how you feel ever better sucking my fingers inside you."

"God, yes. Please. Now." She squirmed against his fingers as he tugged her panties to the side. Trim curls tickled his fingers as he found her slick, already wet and swollen for him. She swallowed a moan as he traced her inner lips, then found her clit, gently circling it before testing a firmer rock of his thumb right there. *Right there.* Jesus H. Murphy, that firm nub against his thumb would be something he'd never forget.

"Arizona, you say," he muttered as he dropped his head to her shoulder, curving his back to make a private space between their bodies. So she could see him touching her, and maybe if she wanted to...

He hissed in a breath as her hands immediately went for his belt. Thank Christ she wanted to.

She fumbled with his dress pants once she had his fly open, because they were loose and if she let go of them, they'd fall. He cursed under his breath and slid his fingers out of her pussy, ignoring her whimper of protest.

"Let me take those off." He stepped back and she pressed her hands to her stomach. Harsh breaths and heavy sighs filled the room, then she laughed. He joined her, because seriously... "I have to warn you, when I take these off, there's going to be a moment when you see me in black dress socks pulled up nearly to my knees. It's not my finest look, so if you want to close your eyes, I understand."

"I don't want to miss a second of this," she whispered, her gaze glued to his face.

Yeah. He knew the feeling. He could still feel her juices on his fingers and—fuck it. He lifted his hand and slid those two fingers into his mouth, tasting her tangy sweetness. Gillian's lips parted, and he wanted to give her a taste, too. Damn it, he needed to lose his pants.

"Fuck," he bit out with a strangled cry, and she laughed again as he hopped around in a stupid circle.

"You're my first debauching closet tour guide."

He jerked his eyes up to her face.

"Just saying. I don't have any other frame of reference, but I think you're doing a bang up job."

"Bang up job." He kicked his pants aside and shoved off his socks, because there was no way he could maintain any cool factor while wearing them. That left him in his shirt, tie, and boxer briefs. Marginally better than with the socks, anyway.

"Key word being bang." She giggled as he fit himself between her spread legs again, hiking her dress high up on her waist. She sighed as he found her wet and ready again, and then her fingers were at his waist and inside his boxers.

Cool fingers wrapped around his cock, the first hand low, nestled right above his balls. She squeezed hard enough to make the blood pump harder and he jerked roughly against her, showing her he liked it. Then her other hand joined in, stroking softly over his sensitive and suspiciously wet head. Great. He was already leaking pre-come. And the combination of hard and soft was a magically good one that made his legs shake and his head go fuzzy.

Why the fuck was Arizona so fucking far away?

"Come here," he muttered, which didn't make any sense because she was pressed against the wall. If he wanted them closer, he needed to lean in. Or maybe he meant that she should leave the sunny dry heat of the desert and visit his debauching closet more often. Jesus, he had no clue. He just needed her to come on his hand and get him off and then promise they'd do it again later.

He'd never looked forward to a wedding quite as much—and didn't care if that made him a turnabout hypocrite.

"You come here," she whispered, tangling their hands together as she stroked him closer and closer to the apex of her curvy, sweet thighs.

The danger zone, because there was nowhere he'd rather come right now.

"I don't have a condom." He was breathing hard and fast now, and his hips moved of their own volition, surging into her sure, firm hand. God. Fucking her would be sweet. But this was good. Twisting his hand, he added another finger as he slid back inside her tight, warm heat. "I want you to come on my hand. You're gonna be so pretty when you come. Fuck, you're the prettiest woman I've ever met, Gillian. Tell me you're gonna do it. Tell me you're close."

"So close." She arched against him, her lips brushing his neck. "You can come on me. I have another dress I can change into."

He huffed a weak laugh. Jesus, this was...fuck. It should be embarrassing or awkward, but it was just hot. Her mouth opened against his skin, her tongue tasting him there, and he shook as the swipe sent sparks skittering through his body.

"Suck harder," he groaned, and she did exactly as he asked, marking his neck as he exploded against her hip, marking her in an even more primal way. She cried out as he shoved against her, sliding his erection through the wet mess he'd just made, and at the same time pressing his body weight against his hand that was still pistoning in and out of her body. The tremor started around his finger tips, the spasming getting stronger as her entire body was overtaken by the orgasm.

He stroked her through it, stretching out her pleasure, until she went limp in his arms. Then he gathered her close and kissed her one last time, savouring the taste of her lips, now devoid of all gloss and even more perfect for it.

"That was…" He braced his forearm against the wall and gave her what he knew was a sloppy grin. He couldn't help it. "That was amazing."

She returned the smile, her entire face lit up with unadulterated pleasure. "It really, really was." She pressed up on her toes and brushed her lips against his. "Thank you. That made a rough weekend truly special."

He knew the feeling. "We should have a dance later."

Her eyes clouded over. "I don't know."

Sam's pulse picked up, and he told it to settle down. "Just a dance. I can contain myself in front of people. Nobody has to know what we did in here."

She nodded. "Right. Sure, maybe we could have a dance."

He stepped back and helped her straighten her dress, painfully aware that she'd be going back to the inn to scrub off the evidence of what they'd just done. He wanted to press his hand to her hip, where he'd spilled his release, and say something deep and meaningful.

But there wasn't anything to say.

Maybe they could have a dance.

Maybe.

But not bloody likely.

7

Some girls went to their wedding in horse-drawn carriages. Others in limos. Mari had always pictured that she'd drive with her dad, though, and that's pretty close to how it ended up.

Her dad and two beefy security guards. If she didn't look in the front seat of the hired SUV they were being driven in, she could pretend this was exactly as she'd imagined as a little girl.

As they approached the winery, her father patted her hand. "Nervous?"

She shook her head. "No...just..."

"This is your life now, sweetheart. And that's okay. It's only different on the outside, ya know?"

A long, slow sigh slipped out. She gripped her bouquet of blue hydrangeas tighter and took an equally slow, restorative inhale.

Her dad kept talking like they were actually having a conversation and she wasn't halfway to emotional zombie land. "Do you feel like yourself on stage?"

"Of course," she whispered.

"Sam doesn't get under your skin then, right?"

She jerked her head away from the window and stared. "You know he's upset?"

"Sweetie, Sam's been upset since his father walked out when he was six. And there's nothing I can do to make that hurt go away. No amount of love fixes that kind of wound. And you gotta know I love him with my whole heart. And so does your mother. But if we can't fix it, you probably can't either."

"We had a fight earlier."

"Something else that you've been doing since you were kids. You always stole his Lego and he'd lose his mind."

"I remember." She half-laughed, half-hiccup cried as she dug into the secret pocket built into her skirt for a tissue.

Her dad waited for her to dab her eyes before continuing, although that was silly because apparently his plan was to rip her heart out. "What you don't remember is that he'd crawl into your toddler bed most nights after you fell asleep and hold you like you were his teddy bear. Like you were the most important thing in his entire world."

Seriously, why had she even bothered hiring a makeup artist? "Dad!"

"Not the time?'" He handed her another tissue and she gave in to the tears.

"No, I think it probably is the time. Obviously we never did this before, so if it just took a wedding to unearth all these feelings, I guess that's good."

"You're his baby sister, and you're eclipsing all of us like a supernova. That's scary."

"That's stupid. I'm not a super anything. I'm just a girl with a guitar."

"Performing in front of thousands of people and marrying a celebrity."

"Chase is hardly—" She cut herself off. For Wardham, he was exactly that. Frankly, for Wardham, so was she, and it was time she stopped hiding from that fact. Dragging in a deep breath, she nodded. "Right. So what do I do?"

"Nothing. Just keep being amazing and give him space to catch up. He's your biggest fan. Well, except for maybe me and your new husband. Maybe."

If she nodded any more, her head would bobble right off.

"You ready?"

With a start, she realized they were sitting outside the entrance to the winery. Stella, Audrey and Karen were standing outside the car with her mother and Chase's mother, and at the door was Sam, with Gavin and Travis right behind him.

Staring out the window at her big brother, she held his

gaze as she smiled and nodded. "Yep. Time for me to get married."

———

SAM CLENCHED his jaw as he opened the door of the SUV, waving off the security dude who thought he had a right to help Sam's sister as she arrived for her wedding. Since he'd returned to the entrance almost an hour earlier, washed up and head mostly on straight—except for the part that was still tangled up in Gillian's skirt, but he could handle that. Compartmentalizing thoughts about soft, womanly skin was something he'd figured out fifteen years earlier.

Now his only concern was making right the terrible wrong he'd committed earlier against the only sister he'd ever have.

"I'm sorry," he said softly but seriously as she took his hand. "You are a queen and this is a celebration worthy of your love."

She snorted and stood on her toes to kiss his cheek. "Wow. Purple prose apology much?"

"The sorry part was authentic."

"I know." She squeezed his hand, and he gave him a smile so regal that the queen comparison wasn't that unrealistic. When had that happened? When had his little sister turned not only into a woman, but one with so much class it hurt to look at her? "Are you walking Mom down the aisle?"

He nodded.

"Then get to it." She stuck her tongue out at him. Okay, regal might be a stretch. "I've got an amazing man to marry."

———

CHASE STOOD, with Davis at his side, at the head of a wide red carpet running between two banks of white folding chairs on the back terrace. The lake shimmered behind them and a perfect late summer breeze was keeping the guests cool. Next to him was the United Church minister, and walking down the aisle was his youngest sister. Behind her waited his oldest sister, then Stella, and while he couldn't see her, he knew Mari was waiting just inside.

A year ago, he'd stepped out back of Danny's to take a phone call and walked back in to Mari dealing with a prick of an ex-boyfriend. Chase had wrapped himself around her, pretending to be her new boyfriend, and from that moment forward, she'd owned him, body, mind, and spirit. She was the sunshine that pulled him out of his bitter shell post-retirement, and her tireless work ethic drove him to be more than just a once-was sports star.

As the music changed and everyone stood up, Chase's heart slammed against his rib cage. Weddings were...whatever. But his wedding? This was something unbelievably special. This moment. The rest of it could fade away, and that would be just fine. As long as he had that woman at the other end of the aisle beaming in his direction, her eyes only for him as his were for her, his life was complete.

She glided toward him on her father's arm, a vision in floating white. Her dress was strapless and simple, and when she got close, he saw it was covered in lace. He raked his gaze over her, soaking up every last detail.

"Sir," he said, dragging his attention to Mark Beadie for a minute. He held out his hand, and Mari's father took it. "Thank you."

"She likes to pretend she doesn't need anyone to take care of her," Mark said gruffly. "She's wrong. Only about that. Nothing else."

Chase grinned. He knew the truth of both of those points quite well. "Yes, sir."

They shook on it, and then her hands were in his, and they were squaring off between their guests and the minister, but the dull roar in Chase's ears meant he missed most of the short address to the assembled well-wishers by the minister and only vaguely registered Carrie Nixon get up and do a reading. Thank God they hired a videographer. He'd have to watch that before his sister could grill him on what his favourite parts were. It would be like watching game tape all over again.

He'd learn the details later. He was pretty sure they were perfect.

She was definitely perfect.

"You look so handsome," she whispered as Davis handed the rings to the minster.

"Did I tell you how beautiful you are?" he asked quietly.

"Like five times since the ceremony started." If her smile got any bigger, he might just die from happiness.

"Good."

They'd gone with pretty standard vows, the same ones his sister had used. All he had to do was repeat after the minister, but he couldn't help but change up the first line a bit.

"My beautiful Mari…" Yeah. That look. So worth every bit of the wedding extravagance for that look as he promised himself to her forever.

"Mari, with all that I am, and all that I have, I vow my life to you.

I will be faithful and honest with you;

I will respect, trust, help and care for you;

And I will share my all with you, whatever may come."

She laced her fingers through his and repeated the same vows back, with her own addition.

"My wonderful Chase. With all that I am, and all that I have, I vow my life to you.

I will be faithful and honest with you;

I will respect, trust, help and care for you;

And I will share my all with you, whatever may come."

As she said the words that would bind them even tighter, she twisted her wrists, gently twining their arms as she swayed against him.

The minister made a joke about getting to the kiss

before they were ready, but it was no laughing matter. Their life together had begun with a kiss—a scorching, soul-melting embrace Chase would remember until his dying day.

He had a lot to live up to, style-wise. And maybe only Mari would know, but since she was the only one that mattered, it still felt like a high standard to meet. And he was ready to not just meet it, but blow it out of the water.

The minister's hand on his shoulder gently eased them apart from their almost kiss, and they exchanged rings so quickly it was probably embarrassing.

"It is now my honour and privilege to pronounce you husband and wife. Chase, you may finally kiss your bride."

He already had her in his arms and her hands were in his hair. Her lips tasted like honey and her breath was hot and sweet. He never wanted to stop kissing her. Would never get enough of the thrill that her tongue gave him every time it slid against his. Of the eager little sounds she made as he deepened the embrace and licked his way inside her mouth, teasing and giving and promising everything under the sun.

He poured everything and then some into the kiss.

Being Mari's husband was the play of a lifetime, and he was going to give it his all.

———

"Can I have this dance?"

Audrey turned around slowly, then clapped her hands together when she saw who was asking. "Heath! You're all dressed up in a suit!"

"Good occasion for it."

"I didn't realize you were here." She nodded toward the dance floor and he moved them in that direction, his hand hovering over the small of her back. In her heels, she was just a few inches shorter than his six-foot-something. It would be nice to dance with a partner that was bigger than her after a series of uncles and smaller cousins that she led around the dance floor.

"I'm sitting at the back with a few other people from high school." He paused a beat. "Nobody you'd remember, probably."

"I—" What did that mean? "I'm sure I would." She frowned at him, but he wasn't looking at her. "Give me some names."

"Nope." He slid her a grin before returning his focus to the band on stage. His hand was sure and warm in the small of her back, and he wasn't doing anything fancy, but he knew how to steer her around the dance floor.

"Why not?"

"Because asking a girl to dance is hard enough. Getting through said dance without an inquisition makes the next dance request that much easier." His lips quirked like he was fighting back a smile.

Audrey tilted her head to the side. "Who else do you want to dance with?"

Now she had his attention. "Pardon?"

"You said, 'it makes asking the next girl that much easier.'" She grinned. "Who else do you want to dance with? Can I help?"

Another frown marred his not-so-baby face, deepening the line between his eyebrows.

"Okay, it's none of my business." She patted him on the shoulder. "You're a decent dancer. I wouldn't worry about anyone turning you down."

He huffed a laugh. "You'd be surprised."

"Well, I'm a woman, and I'm telling you...you've grown up, Heath. You're definitely datable now." Her hand was still curved around the broad bunch of his shoulder muscle. She squeezed. "If I can play wingman, just let me know. Davis can attest to my skills in getting digits."

He slowed to a stop in the centre of the dance floor. "Digits."

"Phone numbers?"

"Yeah, I know—Jesus, Audrey, just how much of a geek do you think I am?"

"I don't think you're a geek." Well, maybe she did, but she'd never *say* that. She frowned at him as he started leading her again, his hand harder on her hip now. Grumpier. Jeez Louise, women might be more obviously emotional, but men and their grumpy funks took top prize for draining behaviour. "This is what you meant when you said you just wanted to dance, no talking, right?"

His hand relaxed on her hip and he turned his head.

His eyes were warmer than she expected, glittering hazel pools that any girl would fall right into. He was crazy if he didn't get that he was totally cute now. But she wasn't going to say that again, because it didn't go over well. He licked his lips and nodded. "Just dancing seems like a good first step."

She nodded, but as he turned her this way and that, his lean body shifting that way and this against hers with little effort, a confused question rocketed around in her brain. What was the second step?

When the song came to an end, they were back where he'd approached her in the first place. He slipped her out of his grasp, like he was releasing a bird to the wild, and stepped back. "Thank you."

"That was fun," she said, taking in the height and breadth of him. "We should dance again before the night is over."

He grinned and gave her a little bow. It was kind of dorky, but that was Heath—he'd always been the class clown, the jokester. Never played anything straight. It was weird to see that in a grown-up man version.

She liked it.

His eyebrows raised as she curtsied in return. Ha. Take that, geek-boy. They'd both changed since high school.

As he disappeared into the partying crowd, she found herself watching for his tall form to reappear, and when it did, she had an interesting feeling form in her chest.

Heath. She'd have to spend more time with him at the bar. That was a friendship worth re-building, she was sure of it.

It wasn't until the end of the night, after they'd all seen Chase and Mari off with balloons and a bridge of mini hockey sticks instead of swords, when the lights came on and they started cleaning up, that she realized they hadn't had another dance.

She stopped in front of the head table, where she'd been putting all the little decorations they'd want to keep into a special box, and looked over at the back corner where he'd been sitting—as far away from the head table as possible—and she rubbed her chest.

"What are you doing?" Stella asked, bumping their shoulders together.

Audrey shook her head and straightened her shoulder. "Nothing."

"It was perfect, Audrey. You did a great job. My hat is off to you. You're a real romantic."

Ha. The truth was so far from that, it was hard not to laugh out loud. But it was late and she was tired and confused. So she nodded and said thanks and tried not to think about missing out on more dancing.

8

"Mrs. Miller, you aren't wearing any clothes."

Mari smoothed her hands down the lace of her wedding dress, now hanging in her closet. She turned her head, her breath catching in her throat at the sight of her husband leaning against the archway between their bedroom and the dressing area. He had a bottle of champagne in one hand, and his tie hung from the other. "I know," she whispered, her mouth suddenly dry. "I, uhm, had fancy underthings, but I've had enough of the fancy trappings for one day."

He moved closer, taking a swig from the bottle before handing it over. The overhead light was off, the only glow in the room coming from a lamp on top of a dresser. They were finally alone. His eyes glittered as he dropped his tie on top of his dresser.

She took a drink.

His hands—big, capable, strong, loving hands, with fingers she wanted to lick and suck and ride—worked at his buttons, baring his chest. The light highlighted his sculpted shoulders and pecs and bounced off the golden curls that bisected his washboard abs.

She took another drink.

"You should help me," he murmured, his lips curling up as she thumped the bottle down a little harder than necessarily and reached for his shirt.

After sliding that off and letting it flutter to the floor, she tucked her fingers over his belt. Warmth from his abdomen tingled through her hands and up her arms. "Mr. Miller, are you going to carry me over the threshold to our marital bed and ravish me?"

"I was thinking more about laying you out on this bench right here and worshipping you like the goddess you are." He stroked his knuckles along her jaw to her ear, then twisted his hand and traced up the sensitive flesh there. "I married a goddess today. Did you know that? It makes me the luckiest man on earth."

"I'm still just a girl who leaves her clothes in a pile on the floor," she whispered, swaying against him as she slid his zipper down and shoved his pants low on his hips. "Or your clothes, I guess. I did hang up my wedding dress."

He chuckled, the sound low and rich in her ear. "I saw that. Gold star."

"Speaking of gold star behaviour, you forgot flutes,"

she murmured against his skin as she licked a line sideways across his pecs.

"Forgot nothing. I'm going to drink the rest of the champagne out of your belly button. And other places."

"That sounds messy."

He laughed. "We're flying out in the morning for Banff and beyond. Honeymoon on the tour bus. I think a bit of sticky champagne residue is the least of our concerns."

"Our tour bus is lovely and clean and not at all like whatever den of masculine depravity you were used to with hockey teams."

With a growl, he picked her up and turned, carrying her through the archway and into their bedroom. "On second thought, *wife*, I think I will take you to bed. Teach you how it's going to be in our marriage."

She shrieked when he dumped her in the middle of the duvet, and was still laughing when he climbed on top of her, suddenly naked. She shoved her hand against his chest. "Oh yeah? How is it going to be?"

"No making fun of hockey, first of all." He lowered himself onto her and bracketed his arms on either side of her head. "Unless you join my pick-up team. Your brothers are all in."

"Go Team Miller. Got it." She scrapped her teeth over the hard cut of his jaw, smooth-shaven for once in his life.

"And there are rules now." He frowned at the burble of laughter that rolled through her. "I'm serious."

"I know. I can't wait to hear what they are."

"No going to bed angry." He rubbed his nose against hers. "No waking up sad. Not even if we're apart."

She knew what he meant. They were blessed. "Do I get to set any rules?"

"As many as you want."

She pulled him closer and ran her lips over the corner of his mouth, breathing in the warmth of his skin and the faint remainder of his aftershave. "This is always home. Right here, between us. We carry it in our hearts and it will be wherever we are."

Catching her lower lip, he sucked gently, a tug that wormed its way through her body and flooded her eager pussy. Damn her body for being so easy for him.

"I've got more," she gasped.

"Anything I haven't heard before?" He ducked his head to her breasts, his movements hurried and hungry now.

"Okay, just one more." Spreading her legs restlessly, she rocked beneath him, simultaneously trying to drive her nipple deeper into his mouth because *oh my God yes*, and at the same time wanting him to move back up her body and just fuck her already. "Crap, I can't remember. Chase!"

"I'm here," he whispered. He stroked up her sides as he rocked against her wet core. Reaching between them, she brought him into her body.

"I love you."

He flexed inside her. "I love you, too. Forever."

They kissed each other, neither of them starting it and

both of them continuing, their mouths echoing what their bodies were doing. Harder, faster. Then slower, when the need built heavy inside and threatened to burst, because neither was ready for this to be over.

Sweaty limbs and murmured whispers. Nonsensical noises that meant nothing and everything, that promised a future full of love just like this.

She clutched at his shoulders as he moved them together, thrusting deeper until he found the spot that made her toes curl and the corners of her vision darken.

She'd loved this man for what felt like ages, and still this was just the start of their life together. She'd loved him with her body more times than she could count, and this was still new and special. It felt like he was pulling her into his body, like they were becoming one, and it wasn't cliched or ridiculous in the least.

God no. She wanted more.

Panting his name, she clung to him as he surged, rough and jerkily, stretching her right to her limits. Beyond, really. She was free falling now, faster faster faster, and then he caught her and together they flew. Higher. The dark turned to bright as every cell in her body exploded in climax.

Holy fucking shit.

Above her, Chase breathed heavily, his forehead pressed hard against hers.

She blinked up at him.

He grinned. "My wife."

She tested her vocal chords. "My husband." Oh good, they still worked.

He laughed and rolled onto his back, pulling her into the crook of his arm.

"We forgot the champagne," she whispered against his sweat-soaked skin.

"Be right back."

She ogled his extra-fine backside as he hopped out of bed and jogged to the dressing area. The recovery time of an athlete was a beautiful, beautiful thing.

Scooting up the bed, she plumped the pillows as he sauntered back. He stole a sip of wine before handing over the bottle.

"So we got married."

She took a sip and giggled. "Yep."

"Favourite part?"

"The speeches." With a happy sigh, she leaned back against the pillows. "Davis was funny. Drunk, but funny."

"He had a flask of rye that he was drinking from all day." Chase shifted onto his elbow and gazed down at her. "I liked your speech. You said a lot of things that resonated with me about staying real and knowing what's important."

"The ceremony was beautiful, too."

He got a funny look on his face.

"What?"

His expression went from chagrined to amused, and he pushed back up to sit. "Gimme the bottle."

She clambered up to sit next to him.

He passed the champagne and took a deep breath. "I totally spaced out during the ceremony. Not like thinking about comic books or anything, but it was...emotional. I got all buzzy headed and all I could see was your face. I didn't expect it to hit me like that."

That was the sweetest thing she'd ever heard. "Baby! I love that." She kissed his shoulder.

"You can't tell anyone. It's not manly."

With a sigh, she wrapped her arm over his shoulder. "Okay. The fact that you're a sensitive, loving human being will remain our dirty little secret."

He turned his head, capturing her mouth with his. Blindly he took the champagne from her and shoved the bottle onto the bedside table.

"What are you doing?" she asked breathlessly as he hauled her into his lap. She straddled his hips, planting her knees on the bed and rising up. So what if they'd just done this? It was their wedding night. He could take her all night long and she'd still want more.

"Refining the definition of sensitive, loving human being," he growled , squeezing her hips and urging her down into his lap.

"Again?" Like there was any question.

He just laughed and kissed her mouth. Yes, again.

THE END

Want more Wardham?

Join my newsletter to get all the Whisper Beach updates — Audrey's book, Stella's book and most definitely Sam's book.

You can also visit my website for links to all the Wardham titles, available on all major ebook retailer sites:

Between Then and Now
What Once Was Perfect
Where Their Hearts Collide
When They Weren't Looking
Beyond Love and Hate
Perfect No Matter What
No Time Like Forever
Beneath These Bright Stars
Forever Begins With a Kiss

And coming soon ...
All That They Desire!

WHAT TO READ NEXT

AN EXCERPT FROM LOVE IN A SMALL TOWN (PINE HARBOUR #1)

HE brought wine and a winning smile. She was in trouble.

"Nope. We're not opening that." She shook her head as he grinned and stepped inside. The temperature outside was dropping and he was wearing a leather jacket she hadn't seen before over jeans and a white t-shirt. He looked good. They didn't need to add alcohol to the mix for her to feel unsteady about what was going to come next.

And it wasn't them, together, in an orgasm-fest for the ages. What happened Friday morning could not be repeated. Not when she'd made up her mind about moving forward with her life in a way that didn't involve Rafe Minelli and his future conquests.

If he wore that jacket around town, there would be a lot of conquests in his near future. Hot damn.

"Then put it on your wine rack or something. I didn't

want to come empty handed." He handed it over but didn't let go right away. He pressed the bottle into her hands and stared at her intently as if he was trying to unlock her secrets.

She was only hiding two things. One she was just trying to work up the courage to share. The other—that he still melted her from the inside out with his chocolate brown eyes and stupid dimple—was locked in the vault.

This wasn't the first time he'd come over since moving out, but it had been at least nine months. He'd taken the Christmas lights down and replaced the weather-stripping on the front door, and she'd given him a stiff thanks at the door. So he hadn't seen—

"You painted."

"Yeah." Because the warm yellow had reminded her too much of him.

"By yourself?" He turned around slowly in her living room, formerly their living room, an inscrutable look on his face.

"It was pretty easy," she muttered. He'd taken half the furniture, which left a lot of room to move stuff around and create bare walls.

"I like the beige." He was totally lying. Taupe, oatmeal, canvas ... didn't matter what she called it, he'd never wanted any neutral colours in their space.

"Have you made any other changes?"

"Uhm, I tiled the backsplash in the kitchen." She pointed the way, which was stupid. They'd bought the house together. He knew where the kitchen was. Had made her coffee in it almost every morning for three years, even if he was gone before she woke up. Had perched her naked on the counter and knelt in front of her, licking—

"Looks good." He glanced back at her, his gaze lingering on her pink cheeks for a moment. "A lot of good memories in here, huh?"

He couldn't know what she was thinking, not exactly, but her breath caught in her throat nonetheless when he patted the counter. "Come here."

She shook her head in short, choppy movements. *Nuh-uh.* They needed space between them. Loads of it.

"I'm not going to bite, Liv." His voice was low and rough, like he was actually promising to bite her all over.

"I'm not so sure about that," she teased as lightly as she could.

He gave her a long, hard look before smiling ruefully. "Yeah, I wouldn't take that bet. So what's for dinner?"

And just like that, the mood shifted. "Beef stroganoff and a salad."

He kept his distance as she worked on the salad, flipping through a newsmagazine on the table. When she pulled a bottle of salad dressing out of the fridge, he moved to take it from her. She noticed the pile of opened mail at the same time he did and cursed under her breath.

"What's this?" He fingered the red flagged letter from the hydro company and she winced.

"It's nothing. I just forgot to pay that bill." She watched as he flipped the letter over and frowned.

"Three months in a row?" The incredulous look on his face told her he didn't buy her excuse. "It says here they're cutting off the power tomorrow."

"I paid it last Wednesday," she mumbled. "It's fine."

"The whole balance?"

No, just the minimum, but he didn't need to know that. "It's fine," she repeated, swiping the mail from the counter and dumping it in the nearest drawer.

He shook his head. "Obviously not. I'll give you some—"

Tight, angry words shot up her throat and she swallowed them back, holding up her hand instead. "No."

"Liv, this is still my house, too. If the costs are too high—"

"Then it's time we sell it. That's the only conversation we're going to have about money, okay?"

He clamped his mouth shut and leaned back against the other counter, crossing his arms. "I don't want to sell."

Even though it was her plan, deep down she didn't want to either. Hot, sweaty memories of the night they moved in flooded her mind unexpectedly and she turned to the sink so he wouldn't see the pink of her cheeks or the bright tears in her eyes.

"Where would you move?"

Pine Harbour didn't have many rental options. Rafe lived in the only apartment building. There were two units above his mother's cafe but that was obviously out of the question, and any house would be out of her price range.

He figured out her plan just as she opened her mouth to confess, and from the sound of his voice at her back, he was pissed. "You're leaving."

"It's for the best," she whispered. She couldn't hang around to see him move on, and it didn't matter that he'd almost kissed her. *Twice, both times acting like you were an oasis in the middle of a freakin' desert.* Didn't matter, she reminded herself, because they'd scorched enough earth in their divorce that really getting back together wasn't going to happen. If they kissed, and oh god did she want that more than her next breath, they'd tumble into bed. And on the other side of a torrid love affair with her ex-husband stood her ex-mother-in-law, ready to brand her as a hussy and drive her out of town.

She wouldn't be pushed. If she left, it would be with her head held high. Rafe needed to not kiss her, end of story, and the only way that was going to happen was if she put some significant geographical distance between them. She cleared her throat and raised her voice enough to claim bravery, however false it might be. "I moved here to be with you. We're not together anymore. It was a mistake to stay after the divorce."

"You have friends here," he rasped, and she wanted to turn and look at him. Wanted to soak up the hungry, needy look she imagined was scrawled across his face and pretend it was enough to pull them back together.

Keep reading Love in a Small Town right now!

THE PINE HARBOUR SERIES
Love in a Small Town
Love in a Snow Storm
Love on a Spring Morning
Love on a Summer Night
Love on the Run
Love in a Sandstorm

Sign up for Zoe's mailing list today!

BOOKS BY ZOE YORK

THE WARDHAM SERIES

Between Then and Now

What Once Was Perfect

Where Their Hearts Collide

When They Weren't Looking

Beyond Love and Hate

Perfect No Matter What

No Time Like Forever

Beneath These Bright Stars

Forever Begins With a Kiss

All That They Desire

PINE HARBOUR

Love in a Small Town

Love in a Snow Storm

Love on a Spring Morning

Love on a Summer Night

Love on the Run

Love in a Sandstorm

SEALS UNDONE

Fall Out

Fall Hard

Fall Away

Fall Deep

Fall Fast

Fall Back

Fall Dark

Fall Dirty

Visit my website and join my mailing list to be the first to hear about new books!

ACKNOWLEDGEMENTS

AKA THE PEOPLE WHO GIVE ME THE CRAZIEST IDEAS

THE first person I need to thank is Kaira Rouda, one of my fellow Inkheart authors, who first suggested the collaborative project that turned into the Love Ever After boxed set (which hit the USA Today bestsellers list the week we released it). Six months later, I'm still grinning about that.

As always, there aren't enough words to properly thank my family, who humour me every single day. And they've stopped being surprised when I say, "So there's a new project I'm involved with..."

Every reader who fell for Sam and Gillian in this book. I'm working on their story.

Every reader who has been waiting for Evan, Jess and Brent's story since early 2014. I'm working on their story, too.

Every reader who has loved Pine Harbour and the

SEALs Undone series, and circled back to Wardham—my first love, my first series, my heart.

Thank you all from the bottom of my soul.

Zoe

ABOUT THE AUTHOR

Zoe York lives in London, Ontario with her young family. She's currently chugging Americanos, wiping sticky fingers, and dreaming of heroes in and out of uniform.

Sign up for my newsletter and get three free reads!!!

Connect with Zoe:
www.zoeyork.com
zoeyorkwrites@gmail.com

* 9 7 8 1 9 2 6 5 2 7 8 3 3 *